Marx Machiavelli Chesterton Emerson Joyce
Abbott Hardy Montaigne Cooper Austen
Defoe Melville Haggard Hugo
Christie Eliot Grimm
Stoker Carroll Molière
Wilde Maupassant Byron
Engels Schiller
Garnett Einstein Fitzgerald Smith
Goethe Hawthorne Kafka
Cotton Dostoyevsky Hall
Baum Kipling Doyle Willis
Leslie Dumas Henry Nietzsche
Flaubert Turgenev Balzac
Stockton Vatsyayana Crane
Burroughs Whitman Verne
Curtis Tocqueville Gogol Vinci
Homer Widger Tolstoy Busch
Darwin Thoreau Scott
Potter Freud Zola Twain Plato
Kant Jowett Lawrence
Stevenson Dickens Harte
Andersen Cervantes Burton Hesse
London Descartes Voltaire
Poe Aristotle Wells
Hale James Hastings Cooke
Bunner Shakespeare Irving
Richter Chambers
Doré Swift Dante Chekhov da Shaw Wodehouse Benedict Alcott
Pushkin
Newton

tredition®

tredition was established in 2006 by Sandra Latusseck and Soenke Schulz. Based in Hamburg, Germany, tredition offers publishing solutions to authors and publishing houses, combined with worldwide distribution of printed and digital book content. tredition is uniquely positioned to enable authors and publishing houses to create books on their own terms and without conventional manufacturing risks.

For more information please visit: www.tredition.com

TREDITION CLASSICS

This book is part of the TREDITION CLASSICS series. The creators of this series are united by passion for literature and driven by the intention of making all public domain books available in printed format again - worldwide. Most TREDITION CLASSICS titles have been out of print and off the bookstore shelves for decades. At tredition we believe that a great book never goes out of style and that its value is eternal. Several mostly non-profit literature projects provide content to tredition. To support their good work, tredition donates a portion of the proceeds from each sold copy. As a reader of a TREDITION CLASSICS book, you support our mission to save many of the amazing works of world literature from oblivion. See all available books at www.tredition.com.

Project Gutenberg

The content for this book has been graciously provided by Project Gutenberg. Project Gutenberg is a non-profit organization founded by Michael Hart in 1971 at the University of Illinois. The mission of Project Gutenberg is simple: To encourage the creation and distribution of eBooks. Project Gutenberg is the first and largest collection of public domain eBooks.

Simon Magus

George Robert Stow Mead

Imprint

This book is part of TREDITION CLASSICS

Author: George Robert Stow Mead
Cover design: Buchgut, Berlin – Germany

Publisher: tredition GmbH, Hamburg - Germany
ISBN: 978-3-8424-4883-4

www.tredition.com
www.tredition.de

SIMON MAGUS

AN ESSAY ON THE FOUNDER OF SIMONIANISM

BASED ON THE ANCIENT SOURCES

WITH A RE-EVALUATION OF HIS PHILOSOPHY AND TEACHINGS.

BY

G.R.S. MEAD

SIMON MAGUS.

INTRODUCTION.

Everybody in Christendom has heard of Simon, the magician, and how Peter, the apostle, rebuked him, as told in the narrative of the *Acts of the Apostles*. Many also have heard the legend of how at Rome this wicked sorcerer endeavoured to fly by aid of the demons, and how Peter caused him to fall headlong and thus miserably perish. And so most think that there is an end of the matter, and either cast their mite of pity or contempt at the memory of Simon, or laugh at the whole matter as the invention of superstition or the imagination of religious fanaticism, according as their respective beliefs may be in orthodoxy or materialism. This for the general. Students of theology and church history, on the other hand, have had a more difficult task set them in comparing and arranging the materials they have at their disposal, as found in the patristic writings and legendary records; and various theories have been put forward, not the least astonishing being the supposition that Simon was an alias for Paul, and that the Simon and Peter in the accounts of the fathers and in the narrative of the legends were simply concrete symbols to represent the two sides of the Pauline and Petrine controversies.

The first reason why I have ventured on this present enquiry is that Simon Magus is invariably mentioned by the heresiologists as the founder of the first heresy of the commonly-accepted Christian era, and is believed by them to have been the originator of those systems of religio-philosophy and theosophy which are now somewhat inaccurately classed together under the heading of Gnosticism. And though this assumption of the patristic heresiologists is entirely incorrect, as may be proved from their own works, it is nevertheless true that Simonianism is the first system that, as far as our present records go, came into conflict with what has been regarded as the orthodox stream of Christianity. A second reason is that I believe that Simon has been grossly misrepresented, and entirely misunderstood, by his orthodox opponents, whoever they were, in the first place, and also, in the second place, by those who have ignorantly and without enquiry copied from them. But my chief reason is that the present revival of theosophical enquiry throws a flood of light on Simon's teachings, whenever we can get anything approaching a first-hand statement of them, and shows that it was identical in its fundamentals with the Esoteric Philosophy of all the great religions of the world.

In this enquiry, I shall have to be slightly wearisome to some of my readers, for instead of giving a selection or even a paraphraze of the notices on Simon which we have from authenticated patristic sources, I shall furnish verbatim translations, and present a digest only of the unauthenticated legends. The growth of the Simonian legend must unfold itself before the reader in its native form as it comes from the pens of those who have constructed it. Repetitions will, therefore, be unavoidable in the marshalling of authorities, but they will be shown to be not without interest in the subsequent treatment of the subject, and at any rate we shall at least be on the sure ground of having before us all that has been said on the matter by the Church fathers. Having cited these authorities, I shall attempt to submit them to a critical examination, and so eliminate all accretions, hearsay and controversial opinions, and thus sift out what reliable residue is possible. Finally, my task will be to show that Simon taught a system of Theosophy, which instead of deserving our condemnation should rather excite our admiration, and that, instead of being a common impostor and impious perverter of public morality, his method was in many respects of the same nature as the methods of the theosophical movement of to-day, and deserves the study and consideration of all students of Theosophy.

This essay will, therefore, be divided into the following parts:

I. —Sources of Information.
II. —A Review of Authorities.
III. —The Theosophy of Simon.

PART I.

SOURCES OF INFORMATION.

Our sources of information fall under three heads: I. The Simon of the *New Testament*; II. The Simon of the Fathers; III. The Simon of the Legends.

I.—*The Simon of the New Testament.*

Acts (viii. 9-24); author and date unknown; commonly supposed to be "by the author of the third gospel, traditionally known as Luke";[1] not quoted prior to A.D. 177;[2] earliest MS. not older than the sixth century, though some contend for the third.

II.—*The Simon of the Fathers.*

i. Justinus Martyr (*Apologia*, I. 26, 56; *Apologia*, II. 15; *Dialogus cum Tryphone*, 120); probable date of First Apology A.D. 141; neither the date of the birth nor death of Justin is known; MS. fourteenth century.

ii. Irenæus (*Contra Hæreses*, I. xxiii. 1-4); chief literary activity last decennium of the second century; MSS. probably sixth, seventh, and eighth centuries; date of birth and death unknown, for the former any time from A.D. 97-147 suggested, for latter 202-3.

iii. Clemens Alexandrinus (*Stromateis*, ii. 11; vii. 17); greatest literary activity A.D. 190-203; born 150-160, date of death unknown; oldest MS. eleventh century.

iv. Tertullianus (*De Præscriptionibus adversus Hæreticos*, 46, generally attributed to a Pseudo-Tertullian); c. A.D. 199; (*De Anima*, 34, 36); c. A.D. 208-9; born 150-160, died 220-240.

v. [Hippolytus (?)] (*Philosophumena*, vi. 7-20); date unknown, probably last decade of second to third of third century; author unknown and only conjecturally Hippolytus; MS. fourteenth century.

vi. Origenes (*Contra Celsum*, i. 57; v. 62; vi. 11); born A.D. 185-6, died 254-5; MS. fourteenth century.

vii. Philastrius (*De Hæresibus*); date of birth unknown, died probably A.D. 387.

viii. Epiphanius (*Contra Hæreses*, ii. 1-6); born A.D. 310-20, died 404; MS. eleventh century.

ix. Hieronymus (*Commentarium in Evangelicum Matthæi*, IV. xxiv. 5); written A.D. 387.

x. Theodoretus (*Hereticarum Fabularum Compendium*, i. 1); born towards the end of the fourth century, died A.D. 453-58; MS. eleventh century.

III. — *The Simon of the Legends.*

A. The so-called Clementine literature.

i. *Recognitiones*, 2. *Homiliæ*, of which the Greek originals are lost, and the Latin translation of Rufinus (born c.A.D. 345, died 410) alone remains to us. The originals are placed by conjecture somewhere about the beginning of the third century; MS. eleventh century.

B. A mediæval account; (*Constitutiones Sanctorum Apostolorum*, VI. vii, viii, xvi); these were never heard of prior to 1546, when a Venetian, Carolus Capellus, printed an epitomized translation of them from an MS. found in Crete. They are hopelessly apocryphal.

I.—*The Simon of the New Testament.*

Acts (viii. 9-24). Text: *The Greek Testament* (with the readings adopted by the revisers of the authorized version); Oxford, 1881.

Now a certain fellow by name Simon had been previously in the city practising magic and driving the people of Samaria out of their wits, saying that he was some great one; to whom all from small to great gave heed, saying: "This man is the Power of God which is called Great." And they gave heed to him, owing to his having driven them out of their wits for a long time by his magic arts. But when they believed on Philip preaching about the Kingdom of God and the Name of Jesus Christ, they began to be baptized, both men and women. And Simon himself also believed, and after being baptized remained constantly with Philip; and was driven out of *his* wits on seeing the signs and great wonders[3] that took place.

And the apostles in Jerusalem hearing that Samaria had received the Word of God, sent Peter and John to them. And they went down and prayed for them, that they might receive the Holy Spirit. For as yet it had not fallen upon any of them, but they had only been baptized unto the Name of the Lord Jesus.

Then they laid their hands on them, and they received the Holy Spirit. And when Simon saw that the Holy Spirit was given by the laying on of the hands of the apostles, he offered them money, saying: "Give unto me also this power, in order that on whomsoever I lay my hands he may receive the Holy Spirit."

But Peter said unto him: "Thy silver perish with thee, in that thou didst think that the gift of God is possessed with money. There is not for thee part or lot in this Word, for thy heart is not right before God. Therefore turn from this evil of thine, and pray the Lord, if by chance the thought of thy heart shall be forgiven thee. For I see that thou art in the gall of bitterness and the bond of iniquity."

And Simon answered and said: "Pray ye on my behalf to the Lord, that none of the things that ye have said may come upon me."

II.—*The Simon of the Fathers.*

i. Justinus Martyr (*Apologia*, I. 26). Text: *Corpus Apologetarum Christianorum Sæculi Secundi* (edidit Io. Car. Th. Eques de Otto); Jenæ, 1876 (ed. tert.).

And thirdly, that even after the ascension of the Christ into heaven the daemons cast before themselves (as a shield) certain men who said that they were gods, who were not only not expelled by you,[4] but even thought worthy of honours; a certain Samaritan, Simon, who came from a village called Gitta; who in the reign of Claudius Cæsar[5] wrought magic wonders by the art of the daemons who possessed him, and was considered a god in your imperial city of Rome, and as a god was honoured with a statue by you, which statue was erected in the river Tiber, between the two bridges, with the following inscription in Roman: "Simoni Deo Sancto." And nearly all the Samaritans, but few among the rest of the nations, confess him to be the first god and worship him. And they speak of a certain Helen, who went round with him at that time, and who had formerly prostituted herself,[6] but was made by him his first Thought.

ii. Irenæus (*Contra Hæreses*, I. xxiii. 1-4). Text: *Opera* (edidit Adolphus Stieren); Lipsiæ, 1848.

1. Simon was a Samaritan, the notorious magician of whom Luke the disciple and adherent of the apostles says: "But there was a fellow by name Simon, who had previously practised the art of magic in their state, and led away the people of the Samaritans, saying that he was some great one, to whom they all listened, from the small to the great, saying: 'He is the Power of God, which is called Great.' Now they gave heed to him because he had driven them out of their wits by his magical phenomena." This Simon, therefore, pretended to be a believer, thinking that the apostles also wrought their cures by magic and not by the power of God; and supposing that their filling with the Holy Spirit by the laying on of hands those who believed in God, through that Christ Jesus who was being preached by them—that this was effected by some superior magical knowledge, and offering money to the apostles, so that he also might obtain the power of giving the Holy Spirit to whomsoever he

would, he received this answer from Peter: "Thy money perish with thee, since thou hast thought that the gift of God is obtained possession of with money; for thee there is neither part nor lot in this Word, for thy heart is not right before God. For I see thou art in the gall of bitterness and the bond of iniquity."

And since the magician still refused to believe in God, he ambitiously strove to contend against the apostles, so that he also might be thought of great renown, by extending his investigations into universal magic still farther, so that he struck many aghast; so much so that he is said to have been honoured with a statue for his magic knowledge by Claudius Cæsar.

He, therefore, was glorified by many as a god; and he taught that it was he himself who, forsooth, appeared among the Jews as the Son, while in Samaria he descended as the Father, and in the rest of the nations he came as the Holy Spirit. That he was the highest power, to wit, the Father over all, and that he allowed himself to be called by whatever name men pleased.

2. Now the sect of the Samaritan Simon, from whom all the heresies took their origin, was composed of the following materials.

He took round with him a certain Helen, a hired prostitute from the Phoenician city Tyre, after he had purchased her freedom, saying that she was the first conception (or Thought) of his Mind, the Mother of All, by whom in the beginning he conceived in his Mind the making of the Angels and Archangels. That this Thought, leaping forth from him, and knowing what was the will of her Father, descended to the lower regions and generated the Angels and Powers, by whom also he said this world was made. And after she had generated them, she was detained by them through envy, for they did not wish to be thought to be the progeny of any other. As for himself, he was entirely unknown by them; and it was his Thought that was made prisoner by the Powers and Angels that has been emanated by her. And she suffered every kind of indignity at their hands, to prevent her reäscending to her Father, even to being imprisoned in the human body and transmigrating into other female bodies, as from one vessel into another.[7] She also was in that Helen, on whose account the Trojan War arose; wherefore also Stesichorus[8] was deprived of his sight when he spake evil of her in his poems; and that afterwards when he repented and wrote what is called a recantation, in which he sang her praises, he recovered his sight. So she, transmigrating from body to body, and thereby also continually undergoing indignity, last of all even stood for hire in a brothel; and she was the "lost sheep."

3. Wherefore also he himself had come, to take her away for the first time, and free her from her bonds, and also to guarantee salvation to men by his "knowledge." For as the Angels were mismanaging the world, since each of them desired the sovereignty, he had come to set matters right; and that he had descended, transforming himself and being made like to the Powers and Principalities and Angels; so that he appeared to men as a man, although he was not a man; and was thought to have suffered in Judæa, although he did not really suffer. The Prophets moreover had spoken their prophecies under the inspiration of the Angels who made the world; wherefore those who believed on him and his Helen paid no further attention to them, and followed their own pleasure as though free; for men were saved by his grace, and not by righteous works. For righteous actions are not according to nature, but from accident, in the manner that the Angels who made the world have laid it down, by such precepts enslaving men. Wherefore also he gave new promises that the world should be dissolved and that they who were his should be freed from the rule of those who made the world.

4. Wherefore their initiated priests live immorally. And everyone of them practises magic arts to the best of his ability. They use exorcisms and incantations. Love philtres also and spells and what are called "familiars" and "dream-senders," and the rest of the curious arts are assiduously cultivated by them. They have also an image of Simon made in the likeness of Jupiter, and of Helen in that of Minerva; and they worship the (statues); and they have a designation from their most impiously minded founder, being called Simonians, from whom the Gnôsis, falsely so-called, derives its origins, as one can learn from their own assertions.

iii. Clemens Alexandrinus (*Stromateis*, ii. 11; vii. 17). Text: *Opera* (edidit G. Dindorfius); Oxoniæ, 1869.

In the first passage the Simonian use of the term, "He who stood," is confirmed, in the latter we are told that a branch of the Simonians was called Entychitæ.

iv. Tertullianus, or Pseudo-Tertullianus (*De Præscriptionibus*, 46). Text: *Liber de Præs.*, etc. (edidit H. Hurter, S.J.); Oeniponti, 1870. Tertullianus (*De Anima*, 34, 36). Text: *Bibliothec. Patr. Eccles. Select.* (curavit Dr. Guil. Bruno Linder), Fasc. iv; Lipsiæ, 1859.

In the *Præscriptions* the passage is very short, the briefest notice possible, under the heading, "Anonymi Catalogus Heresum." The notice in the *De Anima* runs as follows:

For Simon the Samaritan also, the purveyor of the Holy Spirit, in the *Acts of the Apostles*, after he had been condemned by himself, together with his money, to perdition, shed vain tears and betook himself to assaulting the truth, as though for the gratification of vengeance. Supported by the powers of his art, for the purpose of his illusions through some power or other, he purchased with the same money a Tyrian woman Helen from a place of public pleasure, a fit commodity instead of the Holy Spirit. And he pretended that he was the highest Father, and that she was his first suggestion whereby he had suggested the making of the Angels and Archangels; that she sharing in this design had sprung forth from the Father, and leaped down into the lower regions; and that there, the design of the Father being prevented, she had brought forth Angelic Powers ignorant of the Father, the artificer of this world; by these she was detained, not according to his intention, lest when she had gone they should be thought to be the progeny of another. And therefore being made subject to every kind of contumely, so that by her depreciation she might not choose to depart, she had sunk to as low as the human form, as though she had had to be restrained by chains of flesh, and then for many ages being turned about through a succession of female conditions, she became also that Helen who proved so fatal to Priam, and after to the eyes of Stesichorus, for she had caused his blindness on account of the insult of his poem, and afterwards had removed it because of her pleasure at his praise. And thus transmigrating from body to body, in the extreme of dishonour she had stood, ticketed for hire, a Helen viler [than her predecessor]. She was, therefore, the "lost sheep," to whom the highest

Father, Simon, you know, had descended. And after she was recovered and brought back, I know not whether on his shoulders or knees, he afterwards had respect to the salvation of men, as it were by the liberation of those who had to be freed from these Angelic Powers, for the purpose of deceiving whom he transformed himself, and pretended that he was a man to men only, playing the part of the Son in Judæa, and that of the Father in Samaria.

v. [Hippolytus (?)] *(Philosophumena,* vi. 7-20). Text: *Refutatio Omnium Hæresium* (ediderunt Lud. Duncker et F.G. Schneidewin); Gottingæ, 1859.

7. I shall, therefore, set forth the system of Simon of Gittha, a village of Samaria, and shall show that it is from him that those who followed[9] him got their inspiration, and that the speculations they venture upon have been of a like nature, though their terminology is different.

This Simon was skilled in magic, and deluding many, partly by the art of Thrasymedes, in the way we have explained above,[10] and partly corrupting them by means of daemons, he endeavoured to deify himself—a sorcerer fellow and full of insanity, whom the apostles confuted in the *Acts*. Far more prudent and modest was the aim of Apsethus, the Libyan, who tried to get himself thought a god in Libya. And as the story of Apsethus is not very dissimilar to the ambition of the foolish Simon, it will not be unseemly to repeat it, for it is quite in keeping with Simon's endeavour.

8. Apsethus, the Libyan, wanted to become a god. But in spite of the greatest exertions he failed to realize his longing, and so he desired that at any rate people should *think* that he had become one; and, indeed, for a considerable time he really did get people to think that such was the case. For the foolish Libyans sacrificed to him as to some divine power, thinking that they were placing their confidence in a voice that came down from heaven.

Well, he collected a large number of parrots and put them all into a cage. For there are a great many parrots in Libya and they mimic the human voice very distinctly. So he kept the birds for some time and taught them to say, "Apsethus is a god." And when, after a long time, the birds were trained and could speak the sentence which he considered would make him be thought to be a god, he opened the cage and let the parrots go in every direction. And the voice of the birds as they flew about went out into all Libya, and their words reached as far as the Greek settlements. And thus the Libyans, astonished at the voice of the birds, and having no idea of the trick which had been played them by Apsethus, considered him to be a god.

But one of the Greeks, correctly surmising the contrivance of the supposed god, not only confuted him by means of the self-same parrots, but also caused the total destruction of this boastful and vulgar fellow. For the Greek caught a number of the parrots and re-taught them to say "Apsethus caged us and made us say, 'Apsethus is a god.'" And when the Libyans heard the recantation of the parrots, they all assembled together of one accord and burnt Apsethus alive.

9. And in the same way we must regard Simon, the magician, more readily comparing him with the Libyan fellow's thus becoming a god. And if the comparison is a correct one, and the fate which the magician suffered was somewhat similar to that of Apsethus, let us endeavour to *re-teach the parrots of Simon*, that he was not Christ, who has stood, stands and will stand, but a man, the child of a woman, begotten of seed, from blood and carnal desire, like other men. And that this is the case, we shall easily demonstrate as our narrative proceeds.

Now Simon in his paraphrasing of the Law of Moses speaks with artful misunderstanding. For when Moses says "God is a fire burning and destroying,"[11] taking in an incorrect sense what Moses said, he declares that Fire is the Universal Principle, not understanding what was said, viz., not that "God is fire," but "a fire burning and destroying." And thus he not only tears to pieces the Law of Moses, but also plunders from Heracleitus the obscure.[12] And Simon states that the Universal Principle is Boundless Power, as follows:

"*This is the writing of the revelation of Voice and Name from Thought, the Great Power, the Boundless. Wherefore shall it be sealed, hidden, concealed, laid in the Dwelling of which the Universal Root is the foundation.*"[13]

And he says that man here below, born of blood, is the Dwelling, and that the Boundless Power dwells in him, which he says is the

Universal Root. And, according to Simon, the Boundless Power, Fire, is not a simple thing, as the majority who say that the four elements are simple have considered fire also to be simple, but that the Fire has a twofold nature; and of this twofold nature he calls the one side the concealed and the other the manifested, (stating) that the concealed (parts) of the Fire are hidden in the manifested, and the manifested produced by the concealed.

This is what Aristotle calls "in potentiality" and "in actuality," and Plato the "intelligible" and "sensible."

And the manifested side of the Fire has all things in itself which a man can perceive of things visible, or which he unconsciously fails to perceive. Whereas the concealed side is everything which one can conceive as intelligible, even though it escape sensation, or which a man fails to conceive.

And generally we may say, of all things that are, both sensible and intelligible, which he designates concealed and manifested, the Fire, which is above the heavens, is the treasure-house, as it were a great Tree, like that seen by Nabuchodonosor in vision, from which all flesh is nourished. And he considers the manifested side of the Fire to be the trunk, branches, leaves, and the bark surrounding it on the outside. All these parts of the great Tree, he says, are set on fire from the all-devouring flame of the Fire and destroyed. But the fruit of the Tree, if its imaging has been perfected and it takes the shape of itself, is placed in the storehouse, and not cast into the Fire. For the fruit, he says, is produced to be placed in the storehouse, but the husk to be committed to the Fire; that is to say, the trunk, which is generated not for its own sake but for that of the fruit.

10. And this he says is what is written in the scripture: "For the vineyard of the Lord Sabaôth is the house of Israel, and a man of Judah a well-beloved shoot."[14] And if a man of Judah is a well-beloved shoot, it is shown, he says, that a tree is nothing else than a man. But concerning its sundering and dispersion, he says, the scripture has sufficiently spoken, and what has been said is sufficient for the instruction of those whose imaging has been perfected, viz.: "All flesh is grass, and every glory of the flesh as the flower of grass. The grass is dried up and the flower thereof falleth, but the speech of the Lord endureth for the eternity (aeon)."[15] Now the

Speech of the Lord, he says, is the Speech engendered in the mouth and the Word (Logos), for elsewhere there is no place of production.

11. To be brief, therefore, the Fire, according to Simon, being of such a nature—both all things that are visible and invisible, and in like manner, those that sound within and those that sound aloud, those which can be numbered and those which are numbered—in the *Great Revelation* he calls it the Perfect Intellectual, as (being) everything that can be thought of an infinite number of times, in an infinite number of ways, both as to speech, thought and action, just as Empedocles[16] says:

"By earth earth we perceive; by water, water; by aether [divine], aether; fire by destructive fire; by friendship, friendship; and strife by bitter strife."

12. For, he says, he considered that all the parts of the Fire, both visible and invisible, possessed perception[17] and a portion of intelligence. The generable cosmos, therefore, was generated from the ingenerable Fire. And it commenced to be generated, he says, in the following way. The first six Roots of the Principle of generation which the generated (*sc.*, cosmos) took, were from that Fire. And the Roots, he says, were generated from the Fire in pairs,[18] and he calls these Roots Mind and Thought, Voice and Name, Reason and Reflection, and in these six Roots there was the whole of the Boundless Power together, in potentiality, but not in actuality. And this Boundless Power he says is He who has stood, stands and will stand; who, if his imaging is perfected while in the six Powers, will be, in essence, power, greatness and completeness, one and the same with the ingenerable and Boundless Power, and not one single whit inferior to that ingenerable, unchangeable and Boundless Power. But if it remain in potentiality only, and its imaging is not perfected, then it disappears and perishes, he says, just as the potentiality of grammar or geometry in a man's mind. For potentiality when it has obtained art becomes the light of generated things, but if it does not do so an absence of art and darkness ensues, exactly as if it had not existed at all; and on the death of the man it perishes with him.

13. Of these six Powers and the seventh which is beyond the six, he calls the first pair Mind and Thought, heaven and earth; and the

male (heaven) looks down from above and takes thought for its co-partner, while the earth from below receives from the heaven the intellectual fruits that come down to it and are cognate with the earth. Wherefore, he says, the Word ofttimes steadfastly contemplating the things which have been generated from Mind and Thought, that is from heaven and earth, says: "Hear, O heaven, and give ear, O earth, for the Lord hath said: I have generated sons and raised them up, but they have set me aside."[19]

And he who says this, he says, is the seventh Power, He who has stood, stands and will stand, for He is the cause of those good things which Moses praised and said they were very good. And (the second pair is) Voice and Name, sun and moon. And (the third) Reason and Reflection, air and water. And in all of these was blended and mingled the Great Power, the Boundless, He who has stood, as I have said.

14. And when Moses says: "(It is) in six days that God made the heaven and the earth, and on the seventh he rested from all his works," Simon arranges it differently and thus makes himself into a god. When, therefore, they (the Simonians) say, that there are three days before the generation of the sun and moon, they mean esoterically Mind and Thought—that is to say heaven and earth—and the seventh Power, the Boundless. For these three Powers were generated before all the others. And when they say "he hath generated me before all the Aeons," the words, he says, are used concerning the seventh Power. Now this seventh Power which was the first Power subsisting in the Boundless Power, which was generated before all the Aeons, this, he says, was the seventh Power, about which Moses says: "And the spirit of God moved over the water," that is to say, he says, the spirit which hath all things in itself, the Image of the Boundless Power, concerning which Simon says: "*The Image from, the incorruptible Form, alone ordering all things.*" For the Power which moves above the water, he says, is generated from an imperishable Form, and alone orders all things.

Now the constitution of the world being with them after this or a similar fashion, God, he says, fashioned man by taking soil from the earth. And he made him not single but double, according to the image and likeness. And the Image is the spirit moving above the water, which, if its imaging is not perfected, perishes together with the world, seeing that it remains only in potentiality and does not become in actuality. And this is the meaning of the Scripture, he says: "Lest we be condemned together with the world."[20] But if its imaging should be perfected and it should be generated from an "indivisible point," as it is written in his *Revelation*, the small shall become great. And this great shall continue for the boundless and changeless eternity (*aeon*), in as much as it is no longer in the process of becoming.[21]

How and in what manner, then, he asks, does God fashion man? In the Garden (Paradise), he thinks. We must consider the womb a Garden, he says, and that this is the "cave," the Scripture tells us when it says: "I am he who fashioned thee in thy mother's womb,"[22] for he would have it written in this way. In speaking of the Garden, he says, Moses allegorically referred to the womb, if we are to believe the Word.

And, if God fashions man in his mother's womb, that is to say in the Garden, as I have already said, the womb must be taken for the Garden, and Eden for the region (surrounding the womb), and the "river going forth from Eden to water the Garden,"[23] for the navel. This navel, he says, is divided into four channels, for on either side of the navel two air-ducts are stretched to convey the breath, and two veins[24] to convey blood. But when, he says, the navel going forth from the region of Eden is attached to the foetus in the epigastric regions, that which is commonly called by everyone the navel[25] ... and the two veins by which the blood flows and is carried from the Edenic region through what are called the gates of the liver, which nourish the foetus. And the air-ducts, which we said were channels for breath, embracing the bladder on either side in the region of the pelvis, are united at the great duct which is called the dorsal aorta. And thus the breath passing through the side doors towards the heart produces the movement of the embryo. For as long as the babe is being fashioned in the Garden, it neither takes nourishment through the mouth, nor breathes through the nostrils. For seeing that it is surrounded by the waters (of the womb), death would instantly supervene, if it took a breath; for it would draw after it the waters and so perish. But the whole (of the foetus) is wrapped up in an envelope, called the amnion, and is nourished through the navel and receives the essence of the breath through the dorsal duct, as I have said.

15. The river, therefore, he says, which goes out of Eden, is divided into four channels, four ducts, that is to say; into four senses of the foetus: sight, (hearing),[26] smelling, taste and touch. For these are the only senses the child has while it is being formed in the Garden.

This, he says, is the law which Moses laid down, and in accordance with this very law each of his books was written, as the titles show. The first book is *Genesis*, and the title of the book, he says, is sufficient for a knowledge of the whole matter. For this *Genesis*, he says, is sight, which is one division of the river. For the world is perceived by sight.

The title of the second book is *Exodus*. For it was necessary for that which is born to travel through the Red Sea, and pass towards the Desert—by Red the blood is meant, he says—and taste the bitter water. For the "bitter," he says, is the water beyond the Red Sea, inasmuch as it is the path of knowledge of painful and bitter things which we travel along in life. But when it is changed by Moses, that is to say by the Word, that bitter (water) becomes sweet. And that this is so, all may hear publicly by repeating after the poets:

"In root it was black, but like milk was the flower. Moly the Gods call it. For mortals to dig it up is difficult; but Gods can do all things."[27]

16. Sufficient, he says, is what is said by the Gentiles for a knowledge of the whole matter, for those who have ears for hearing. For he who tasted this fruit, he says, was not only not changed into a beast by Circe, but using the virtue of the fruit, reshaped those who had been already changed into beasts, into their former proper shape, and re-struck and recalled their type. For the true man and one beloved by that sorceress is discovered by this milk-white divine fruit, he says.

In like manner *Leviticus*, the third book, is smelling or respiration. For the whole of that book treats of sacrifices and offerings. And wherever there is a sacrifice, there arises the smell of the scent from the sacrifice owing to the incense, concerning which sweet smell the sense of smell is the test.

Numbers, the fourth book, signifies taste, wherein speech (or the Word) energizes. And it is so called through uttering all things in numerical order.

Deuteronomy, again, he says, is so entitled in reference to the sense of touch of the child which is formed. For just as the touch by contact synthesizes and confirms the sensations of the other senses, proving objects to be either hard, warm, or adhesive, so also the fifth book of the Law is the synthesis of the four books which precede it.

All ingenerables, therefore, he says, are in us in potentiality but not in actuality, like the science of grammar or geometry. And if they meet with befitting utterance[28] and instruction, and the "bitter" is turned into the "sweet"—that is to say, spears into reaping hooks and swords into ploughshares[29]—the Fire will not have born to it husks and stocks, but perfect fruit, perfected in its imaging, as I said above, equal and similar to the ingenerable and Boundless Power. "For now," says he, "the axe is nigh to the roots of the tree: every tree," he says, "that bringeth not forth good fruit, is cut down and cast into the fire."[30]

17. And so, according to Simon, that blessed and imperishable (principle) concealed in everything, is in potentiality, but not in actuality, which indeed is He who has stood, stands and will stand; who has stood above in the ingenerable Power, who stands below in the stream of the waters, generated in an image, who shall stand above, by the side of the blessed and Boundless Power, if the imaging be perfected. For three, he says, are they that stand, and without there being three standing Aeons, there would be no setting in order[31] of the generable which, according to them, moves on the water, and which is fashioned according to the similitude into a perfect celestial, becoming in no whit inferior to the ingenerable Power, and this is the meaning of their saying: "*Thou and I, the one thing; before me, thou; that after thee, I.*"

This, he says, is the one Power, separated into the above and below, generating itself, increasing itself, seeking itself, finding itself, its own mother, its own father, its sister, its spouse; the daughter, son, mother, and father of itself; One, the Universal Root.

And that, as he says, the beginning of the generation of things which are generated is from Fire, he understands somewhat in this fashion. Of all things of which there is generation, the beginning of the desire for their generation is from Fire. For, indeed, the desire of mutable generation is called "being on fire." And though Fire is one, yet has it two modes of mutation. For in the man, he says, the blood, being hot and yellow—like fire when it takes form—is turned into seed, whereas in the woman the same blood (is changed) into milk. And this change in the male becomes the faculty of generating, while that in the female (becomes) nourishment for the child. This, he says, is "the flaming sword that is turned about to keep the way of the tree of life."[32] For the blood is turned into seed and milk; and this Power becomes mother and father, father of those that are born, and mother of those that are nourished, standing in want of nothing, sufficient unto itself. And the tree of life, he says, is guarded by the fiery sword which is turned about, (which tree), as we have said, (is) the seventh Power which proceeds from itself, contains all (in itself), and is stored in the six Powers. For were the flaming sword not turned about, that fair tree would be destroyed and perish; but if it is turned into seed and milk, that which is stored in them in potentiality, having obtained a fitting utterance,[33] and an appointed place in which the utterance may be developed, starting as it were from the smallest spark, it will increase to all perfection, and expand, and be an infinite power, unchangeable, equal and similar to the unchangeable Aeon, which is no more generated for the boundless eternity.

18. Conformably, therefore, to this reasoning, for the foolish, Simon was a god, like that Libyan Apsethus; (a god) subject to generation and suffering, so long as he remained in potentiality, but freed from the bonds of suffering and birth, as soon as his imaging forth was accomplished, and attaining perfection he passed forth from the first two Powers, to wit heaven and earth. For Simon speaks distinctly concerning this in his *Revelation* as follows:

"To you, therefore, I say what I say, and write what I write. And the writing is this.

"Of the universal Aeons there are two shoots, without beginning or end, springing from one Root, which is the Power invisible, inapprehensible Silence. Of these shoots one is manifested from above, which is the Great Power, the Universal Mind ordering all things, male, and the other, (is manifested) from below, the Great Thought, female, producing all things.

"Hence pairing with each other,[34]*they unite and manifest the Middle Distance, incomprehensible Air, without beginning or end. In this is the Father who sustains all things, and nourishes those things which have a beginning and end.*

"This is He who has stood, stands and will stand, a male-female power like the preëxisting Boundless Power, which has neither beginning nor end, existing in oneness. For it is from this that the Thought in the oneness proceeded and became two.

"So he[35]*was one; for having her*[36]*in himself, he was alone, not however first, although preëxisting, but being manifested from himself to himself, he became second. Nor was he called Father before (Thought) called him Father.*

"As, therefore, producing himself by himself, he manifested to himself his own Thought, so also the Thought that was manifested did not make the Father, but contemplating him hid him – that is to say the Power – in herself, and is male-female, Power and Thought.

"Hence they pair with each other being one, for there is no difference between Power and Thought. From the things above is discovered Power, and from those below Thought.

"In the same manner also that which was manifested from them[37]*although being one is yet found as two, the male-female having the female in itself. Thus Mind is in Thought – things inseparable from one another – which although being one are yet found as two."*

19. So then Simon by such inventions got what interpretation he pleased, not only out of the writings of Moses, but also out of those of the (pagan) poets, by falsifying them. For he gives an allegorical interpretation of the wooden horse, and Helen with the torch, and a number of other things, which he metamorphoses and weaves into fictions concerning himself and his Thought.

And he said that the latter was the "lost sheep," who again and again abiding in women throws the Powers in the world into confusion, on account of her unsurpassable beauty; on account of which the Trojan War came to pass through her. For this Thought took up its abode in the Helen that was born just at that time, and thus when all the Powers laid claim to her, there arose faction and war among those nations to whom she was manifested.

It was thus, forsooth, that Stesichorus was deprived of sight when he abused her in his verses; and afterwards when he repented and wrote the recantation in which he sung her praises he recovered his sight.

And subsequently, when her body was changed by the Angels and lower Powers—which also, he says, made the world—she lived in a brothel in Tyre, a city of Phoenicia, where he found her on his arrival. For he professes that he had come there for the purpose of finding her for the first time, that he might deliver her from bondage. And after he had purchased her freedom he took her about with him, pretending that she was the "lost sheep," and that he himself was the Power which is over all. Whereas the impostor having fallen in love with this strumpet, called Helen, purchased and kept her, and being ashamed to have it known by his disciples, invented this story.

And those who copy the vagabond magician Simon do like acts, and pretend that intercourse should be promiscuous, saying: "All soil is soil, and it matters not where a man sows, so long as he does sow." Nay, they pride themselves on promiscuous intercourse, saying that this is the "perfect love," citing the text, "the holy shall be sanctified by the ... of the holy."[38] And they profess that they are not in the power of that which is usually considered evil, for they are redeemed. For by purchasing the freedom of Helen, he (Simon) thus offered salvation to men by knowledge peculiar to himself.[39]

For he said that, as the Angels were misgoverning the world owing to their love of power, he had come to set things right, being metamorphosed and made like unto the Dominions, Principalities and Angels, so that he was manifested as a man although he was not really a man, and that he seemed to suffer[40] in Judæa, although he did not really undergo it, but that he was manifested to the Jews as the Son, in Samaria as the Father, and among the other nations as the Holy Ghost, and that he permitted himself to be called by whatever name men pleased to call him. And that it was by the Angels, who made the world, that the Prophets were inspired to utter their prophecies. Wherefore they who believe on Simon and Helen pay no attention to the latter even to this day, but do everything they like, as being free, for they contend that they are saved through his (Simon's) grace.

For (they assert that) there is no cause for punishment if a man does ill, for evil is not in nature but in institution. For, he says, the Angels who made the world, instituted what they wished, thinking by such words to enslave all who listened to them. Whereas the dissolution of the world, they (the Simonians) say, is for the ransoming of their own people.

20. And (Simon's) disciples perform magical ceremonies and (use) incantations, and philtres and spells, and they also send what are called "dream-sending" daemons for disturbing whom they will. They also train what are called "familiars,"[41] and have a statue of Simon in the form of Zeus, and one of Helen in the form of Athena, which they worship, calling the former Lord and the latter Lady. And if any among them on seeing the images, calls them by the name of Simon or Helen, he is cast out as one ignorant of the mysteries.

While this Simon was leading many astray by his magic rites in Samaria, he was confuted by the apostles. And being cursed, as it is written in the *Acts*, in dissatisfaction took to these schemes. And at last he travelled to Rome and again fell in with the apostles, and Peter had many encounters with him for he continued leading numbers astray by his magic. And towards the end of his career going ... he settled under a plane tree and continued his teachings. And finally running the risk of exposure through the length of his stay, he said, that if he were buried alive, he would rise again on the third day. And he did actually order a grave to be dug by his disciples and told them to bury him. So they carried out his orders, but he has stopped away[42] until the present day, for he was not the Christ.

vi. Origenes (*Contra Celsum,* i. 57; v. 62; vi. ii). Text (edidit Carol. Henric. Eduard); Lommatzsch; Berolini, 1846.

i. 57. And Simon also, the Samaritan magician, endeavoured to steal away certain by his magic. And at that time he succeeded in deceiving them, but in our own day I do not think it possible to find thirty Simonians altogether in the inhabited world. And probably I have said more than they really are. There are a very few of them round Palestine; but in the rest of the world his name is nowhere to be found in the sense of the doctrine he wished to spread broadcast concerning himself. And alongside of the reports about him, we have the account from the *Acts*. And they who say these things about him are Christians and their clear witness is that Simon was nothing divine.

v. 62. Then pouring out a quantity of our names, he (Celsus) says he knows certain Simonians who are called Heleniani, because they worship Helen or a teacher Helenus. But Celsus is ignorant that the Simonians in no way confess that Jesus is the Son of God, but they say that Simon is the Power of God, telling some marvellous stories about the fellow, who thought that if he laid claim to like powers as those which he thought Jesus laid claim to, he also would be as powerful among men as Jesus is with many.

vi. ii. For the former (Simon) pretended he was the Power of God, which is called Great, and the latter (Dositheus) that he too was the Son of God. For nowhere in the world do the Simonians any longer exist. Moreover by getting many under his influence Simon took away from his disciples the danger of death, which Christians were taught was taken away, teaching them that there was no difference between it and idolatry. And yet in the beginning the Simonians were not plotted against. For the evil daemon who plots against the teaching of Jesus, knew that no counsel of his own would be undone by the disciples of Simon.

vii. Philastrius (*De Hæresibus*, i). Text: *Patres Quarti Ecclesiæ Sæculi* (edidit D.A.B. Caillau); Paris, 1842.

Now after the passion of Christ, our Lord, and his ascension into heaven, there arose a certain Simon, the magician, a Samaritan by birth, from a village called Gittha, who having the leisure necessary for the arts of magic deceived many, saying that he was some Power of God, above all powers. Whom the Samaritans worship as the Father, and wickedly extol as the founder of their heresy, and strive to exalt him with many praises. Who having been baptized by the blessed apostles, went back from their faith, and disseminated a wicked and pernicious heresy, saying that he was transformed supposedly, that is to say like a shadow, and thus he had suffered, although, he says, he did not suffer.

And he also dared to say that the world had been made by Angels, and the Angels again had been made by certain endowed with perception from heaven, and that they (the Angels) had deceived the human race.

He asserted, moreover, that there was a certain other Thought, who descended into the world for the salvation of men; he says she was that Helen whose story is celebrated in the Trojan War by the vain-glorious poets. And the Powers, he says, led on by desire of this Helen, stirred up sedition. "For she," he says, "arousing desire in those Powers, and appearing in the form of a woman, could not reäscend into heaven, because the Powers which were in heaven did not permit her to reascend." Moreover, she looked for another Power, that is to say, the presence of Simon himself, which would come and free her.

The wooden horse also, which the vain-glorious poets say was in the Trojan War, he asserted was allegorical, namely, that that mechanical invention typified the ignorance of all the impious nations, although it is well known that that Helen, who was with the magician, was a prostitute from Tyre, and that this same Simon, the magician, had followed her, and together with her had practised various magic arts and committed divers crimes.

But after he had fled from the blessed Peter from the city of Jerusalem, and came to Rome, and contended there with the blessed apostle before the Emperor Nero, he was routed on every point by the speech of the blessed apostle, and being smitten by an angel came by a righteous end in order that the glaring falsity of his magic might be made known unto all men.

viii. Epiphanius (*Contra Hæreses*, ii. 1-6). Text: *Opera* (edidit G. Dindorfius); Lipsiæ, 1859.

1. From the time of Christ to our own day the first heresy was that of Simon the magician, and though it was not correctly and distinct-

ly one of the Christian name, yet it worked great havoc by the corruption it produced among Christians. This Simon was a sorcerer, and the base of his operations was at Gittha, a city in Samaria, which still exists as a village. And he deluded the Samaritan people with magical phenomena, deluding and enticing them with a bait by saying that he was the Great Power of God and had come down from above. And he told the Samaritans that he was the Father, and the Jews that he was the Son, and that in undergoing the passion he had not really done so, but that it was only in appearance. And he ingratiated himself with the apostles, was baptized by Philip with many others, and received the same rite as the rest. And all except himself awaited the arrival of the great apostles and by the laying on of their hands received the Holy Spirit, for Philip, being a deacon, had not the power of laying on of hands to grant thereby the gift of the Holy Spirit. But Simon, with wicked heart and erroneous calculations, persisted in his base and mercenary covetousness, without abandoning in any way his miserable pursuits, and offered money to Peter, the apostle, for the power of bestowing the Holy Spirit by the laying on of hands, calculating that he would give little, and that for the little (he gave), by bestowing the Spirit on many, he would amass a large sum of money and make a profit.

2. So with his mind in a vile state through the devilish illusions produced by his magic, and weaving all kinds of images, and being ever ready of his own villany to show his barbaric and demoniacal tricks by means of his charms, he came forward publicly and under the cloak of the name of Christ; and pretending that he was mixing hellebore[43] with honey, he added a poison for those whom he hunted into his mischievous illusion, under the cloak of the name of Christ, and compassed the death of those who believed. And being lewd in nature and goaded on through shame of his promises, the vagabond fabricated a corrupt allegory for those whom he had deceived. For picking up a roving woman, called Helen, who originated from the city of the Tyrians, he took her about with him, without letting people know that he was on terms of undue intimacy with her; and when he was involved in bursting disgrace because of his mistress, he started a fabulous kind of psychopompy[44] for his disciples, and saying, forsooth, that he was the Great Power of God, he ventured to call his prostitute companion the Holy Spirit, and he

says that it was on her account he descended. "And in each heaven I changed my form," he says, "in order that I might not be perceived by my Angelic Powers, and descend to my Thought, which is she who is called Prunîcus[45] and Holy Spirit, through whom I brought into being the Angels, and the Angels brought into being the world and men." (He claimed) that this was the Helen of old, on whose account the Trojans and Greeks went to war. And he related a myth with regard to these matters, that this Power descending from above changed its form, and that it was about this that the poets spake allegorically. And through this Power from above—which they call Prunîcus, and which is called by other sects Barbero or Barbelo—displaying her beauty, she drove them to frenzy, and on this account was she sent for the despoiling of the Rulers who brought the world into being; and the Angels themselves went to war on her account; and while she experienced nothing, they set to work to mutually slaughter each other on account of the desire which she infused into them for herself. And constraining her so that she could not reäscend, each had intercourse with her in every body of womanly and female constitution—she reïncarnating from female bodies into different bodies, both of the human kingdom, and of beasts and other things—in order that by means of their slaying and being slain, they might bring about a diminution of themselves through the shedding of blood, and that then she by collecting again the Power would be enabled to reäscend into heaven.

3. And she it was at that time who was possessed by the Greeks and Trojans; and that both in the night of time before the world existed, and after its existence, by the invisible Powers she had wrought things of a like nature. "And she it is who is now with me, and on her account have I descended. And she was looking for my coming. For she is the Thought,[46] called Helen in Homer." And it was on this account that Homer was compelled to portray her as standing on a tower, and by means of a torch revealing to the Greeks the plot of the Phrygians. And by the torch, he delineated, as I said, the manifestation of the light from above. On which account also the wooden horse in Homer was devised, which the Greeks think was made for a distinct purpose, whereas the sorcerer maintained that this is the ignorance of the Gentiles, and that like as the Phrygians when they dragged it along in ignorance drew on their

own destruction, so also the Gentiles, that is to say people who are "without my wisdom," through ignorance, draw ruin on themselves. Moreover the impostor said that Athena again was identical with what they called Thought, making use forsooth of the words of the holy apostle Paul—changing the truth into his own lie—to wit: "Put on the breastplate of faith and the helmet of salvation, and the greaves and sword and buckler";[47] and that all this was in the mimes of Philistion,[48] the rogue!—words uttered by the apostle with firm reasoning and faith of holy conversation, and the power of the divine and heavenly word—turning them further into a joke and nothing more. For what does he say? That he (Philistion) arranged all these things in a mysterious manner into types of Athena. Wherefore again, in making known the woman with him whom he had taken from Tyre and who had the same name as Helen of old, he spoke as I have told you above, calling her by all those names, Thought, and Athena, and Helen and the rest. "And on her account," he says, "I descended. And this is the 'lost sheep' written of in the Gospel." Moreover, he left to his followers an image, his own presumably, and they worship it under the form of Zeus; and he left another in like manner of Helen in the guise of Athena, and his dupes worship them.

4. And he enjoined mysteries of obscenity and—to set it forth more seriously—of the sheddings of bodies, *emissionum virorom, feminarum menstruorum*, and that they should be gathered up for mysteries in a most filthy collection; that these were the mysteries of life, and of the most perfect Gnôsis—a practice which anyone who has understanding from God would most naturally consider to be most filthy conduct and death rather than life. And he supposes names for the Dominions and Principalities, and says there are different heavens, and sets forth Powers for each firmament and heaven, and tricks them out with barbarous names, and says that no man can be saved in any other fashion than by learning this mystagogy, and how to offer such sacrifices to the Universal Father through these Dominions and Principalities. And he says that this world (aeon) was constructed defectively by Dominions and Principalities of evil. And he considers that corruption and destruction are of the flesh alone, but that there is a purification of souls and that, only if they are established in initiation by means of his misleading Gnôsis.

This is the beginning of the so-called Gnostics. And he pretended that the Law was not of God, but of the left-hand Power, and that the Prophets were not from the Good God but from this or the other Power. And he lays it down for each of them as he pleases: the Law was of one, David of another, Isaiah of another, Ezekiel again of another, and ascribes each of the Prophets to some one Dominion. And all of them were from the left-hand Power and outside the Perfection,[49] and every one that believed in the *Old Testament* was subject to death.

5. But this doctrine is overturned by the truth itself. For if he were the Great Power of God, and the harlot with him the Holy Spirit, as he himself says, let him say what is the name of the Power or in what word[50] he discovered the epithet for the woman and nothing for himself at all. And how and at what time is he found at Rome successively paying back his debt, when in the midst of the city of the Romans the miserable fellow fell down and died? And in what scripture did Peter prove to him that he had neither lot nor share in the heritage of the fear of God? And could the world not have its existence in the Good God, when all the good were chosen by him? And how could it be a left-hand Power which spake in the Law and Prophets, when it has preached the coming of the Christ, the Good God, and forbids mean things? And how could there not be one divine nature and the same spirit of the *New* and *Old Testament*, when the Lord said: "I am not come to destroy the Law, but to fulfil it"?[51] And that He might show that the Law was declared through Him and was given through Moses, and that the grace of the Gospel has been preached through himself and his carnal presence, He said to the Jews: "If ye believe Moses, ye should also believe me; for he wrote about me."[52] There are many other arguments also to oppose to the contention of the sorcerer. For how will obscene things give life, if it were not a conception of daemons? When the Lord himself answers in the Gospel to those who say unto him: "If such is the case of the man and the woman, it is not good to marry." But He said unto them: "All do not hold this; for there are eunuchs who made themselves eunuchs for the sake of the kingdom of the heavens."[53] And He showed that natural abstinence from union is the gift of the kingdom of the heavens; and again in another place He says with respect to righteous marriage—which Simon of his own

accord basely corrupting treats according to his own desires—"Whom God has joined together let no man put asunder."[54]

6. And how unaware is again the vagabond that he confutes himself by his own babbling, not knowing what he gives out? For after saying that the Angels were produced by him through his Thought, he goes on to say that he changed his form in every heaven, to escape their notice in his descent. Consequently he avoided them through fear. And how did the babbler fear the Angels whom he had himself made? And how will not the dissemination of his error be found by the intelligent to be instantly refuted by everyone, when the scripture says: "In the beginning[55] God made the heaven and the earth"?[56] And in unison with this word, the Lord in the Gospel says, as though to his own Father: "O Father, Lord of heaven and earth."[57] If, therefore, the maker of heaven and earth is naturally God, the Father of our Lord Jesus Christ, all that the slanderer Simon says is vain; to wit, the defective production of the world by the Angels, and all the rest he has babbled about in addition to his world of Daemons, and he has deceived those who have been led away by him.

ix. Hieronymus (In *Matthaeum*, IV. xxiv. 5). Text: *S. Eusebii Hieronymi Comment.*; Migne *Patrol. Grec.*, VII. col. 176.

Of whom there is one Simon, a Samaritan, whom we read of in the *Acts of the Apostles*, who said he was some Great Power. And among the rest of the things written in his volumes, he proclaimed as follows:

"I am the Word of God; I am the glorious one, I the Paraclete, the Almighty, I the whole of God."

x. Theodoretus *(Hæreticarum Fabularum Compendium,* I. i.). Text: *Opera Omnia* (ex recensione Jacobi Simondi, denuo edidit Joann. Ludov. Schulze); Halæ, 1769.

Now Simon, the Samaritan magician, was the first minister of his (the Daemon's)[58] evil practices who arose. Who, making his base of operations from Gittha, which is a village of Samaria, and having rushed to the height of sorcery, at first persuaded many, by the wonder-working he wrought, to attend his school, and call him some divine Power. But afterwards seeing the apostles accomplishing wonder-workings that were really true and divine, and bestowing on those who came to them the grace of the Spirit, thinking himself also worthy to receive equal power from them, when great Peter detected his villainous intention, and bade him heal the incurable wounds of his mind with the drugs of repentance, he immediately returned to his former evil-doing, and leaving Samaria, since it had received the seeds of salvation, ran off to those who had not yet been tilled by the apostles, in order that, having deceived with his magic arts those who were easy to capture, and having enslaved them in the bonds of their own legendary lore,[59] he might make the teachings of the apostles difficult to be believed.

But the divine grace armed great Peter against the fellow's madness. For following after him, he dispelled his abominable teaching like mist and darkness, and showed forth the rays of the light of truth. But for all that the thrice wretched fellow, in spite of his public exposure, did not cease from his working against the truth, until he came to Rome, in the reign of Claudius Cæsar. And he so astonished the Romans with his sorceries that he was honoured with a brazen pillar. But on the arrival of the divine Peter, he stripped him naked of his wings of deception, and finally, having challenged him to a contest in wonder-working, and having shown the difference between the divine grace and sorcery, in the presence of the assembled Romans, caused him to fall headlong from a great height by his prayers and captured the eye-witnesses of the wonder for salvation.

This (Simon) gave birth to a legend somewhat as follows. He started with supposing some Boundless Power; and he called this the Universal Root.[60] And he said that this was Fire, which had a twofold energy, the manifested and the concealed. The world moreover was generable, and had been generated from the manifested energy of the Fire. And first from it (the manifested energy) were emanated three pairs, which he also called Roots. And the first (pair) he called Mind and Thought, and the second, Voice and Intelligence, and the third, Reason and Reflection. Whereas he called himself the Boundless Power, and (said) that he had appeared to the Jews as the Son, and to the Samaritans he had descended as the Father, and among the rest of the nations he had gone up and down as the Holy Spirit.

And having made a certain harlot, who was called Helen, live with him, he pretended that she was his first Thought, and called her the Universal Mother, (saying) that through her he had made both the Angels and Archangels; and that the world was fabricated by the Angels. Then the Angels in envy cast her down among them, for they did not wish, he says, to be called fabrications. For which cause, forsooth, they induced her into many female bodies and into that of the famous Helen, through whom the Trojan War arose.

It was on her account also, he said, that he himself had descended, to free her from the chains they had laid upon her, and to offer to men salvation through a system of knowledge peculiar to himself.

And that in his descent he had undergone transformation, so as not to be known to the Angels that manage the establishment of the world. And that he had appeared in Judæa as a man, although he was not a man, and that he had suffered, though not at all suffering, and that the Prophets were the ministers of the Angels. And he admonished those that believed on him not to pay attention to them, and not to tremble at the threats of the Law, but, as being free, to do whatever they would. For it was not by good actions, but by grace they would gain salvation.

For which cause, indeed, those of his association ventured on every kind of licentiousness, and practised every kind of magic, fabricating love philtres and spells, and all the other arts of sorcery, as though in pursuit of divine mysteries. And having prepared his (Simon's) statue in the form of Zeus, and Helen's in the likeness of Athena, they burn incense and pour out libations before them, and worship them as gods, calling themselves Simonians.

III.—*The Simon of the Legends.*

The so-called Clementine Literature:

A. *Recognitiones.* Text: Rufino Aquilei Presb. Interprete (curante E.G. Gersdorf); Lipsiæ, 1838.

Homiliæ. Text: *Bibliotheca Patrum Ecclesiasticorum Latinorum Selecta,* Vol. I. (edidit Albertus Schwegler); Tubingensis, Stuttgartiæ, 1847.

B. *Constitutiones.* Text: *SS. Patrum qui Temporibus Apostolicis Floruerunt Opera* (edidit J.B. Cotelerius); Amsteladami, 1724.

A. The priority of the two varying accounts, in the *Homilies* and *Recognitiones,* of the same story is in much dispute, but this is a question of no importance in the present enquiry. The latest scholarship is of the opinion that "the Clementines are unmistakably a production of the sect of the Ebionites."[61] The Ebionites are described as:

A sect of heretics developed from among the Judaizing Christians of apostolic times late in the first or early in the second century. They accepted Christianity only as a reformed Judaism, and believed in our Blessed Lord only as a mere natural man spiritually perfected by exact observance of the Mosaic law.[62]

Summary.[63] Clement, the hero of the legendary narrative, arrives at Cæsarea Stratonis in Judæa, on the eve of a great controversy between Simon and the apostle Peter, and attaches himself to the latter as his disciple (H. II. xv; R.I. lxxvii). The history of Simon is told to Clement, in the presence of Peter, by Aquila and Nicetas—the adopted sons of a convert—who had associated with Simon.

Simon was the son of Antonius and Rachael, a Samaritan of Gittha, a village six schoeni[64] from the city of Cæsarea (H.I. xxii), called a village of the Gettones (R. II. vii). It was at Alexandria that Simon perfected his studies in magic, being an adherent of John, a Hemero-baptist,[65] through whom he came to deal with religious doctrines.

John was the forerunner of Jesus, according to the method of combination or coupling.[66] Whereas Jesus had twelve disciples, as the Sun, John, the Moon, had thirty, the number of days in a lunation, or more correctly twenty-nine and a half, one of his disciples being a woman called Helen, and a woman being reckoned as half a man in the perfect number of the Triacontad, or Plerôma of the Aeons (H.I. xxiii; R. II. viii). In the *Recognitions* the name of Helen is given as Luna in the Latin translation of Rufinus.[67]

Of all John's disciples, Simon was the favourite, but on the death of his master, he was absent in Alexandria, and so Dositheus,[68] a co-disciple, was chosen head of the school.

Simon, on his return, acquiesced in the choice, but his superior knowledge could not long remain under a bushel. One day Dositheus, becoming enraged, struck at Simon with his staff; but the staff passed through Simon's body like smoke, and Dositheus, struck with amazement, yielded the leadership to Simon and became his disciple, and shortly afterwards died (H.I. xxiv; R. II. xiii).

Aquila and Nicetas then go on to tell how Simon had confessed to them privately his love for Luna (R. II. viii), and narrate the magic achievements possessed by Simon, of which they have had proof with their own eyes. Simon can dig through mountains, pass through rocks as if they were merely clay, cast himself from a lofty mountain and be borne gently to earth, can break his chains when in prison, and cause the doors to open of their own accord, animate statues and make the eye-witness think them men, make trees grow suddenly, pass through fire unhurt, change his face or become double-faced, or turn into a sheep or goat or serpent, make a beard grow upon a boy's chin, fly in the air, become gold, make and unmake kings, have divine worship and honours paid him, order a sickle to go and reap of itself and it reaps ten times as much as an ordinary sickle (R. II. xi).

To this list of wonders the *Homilies* add making stones into loaves, melting iron, the production of images of all kinds at a banquet; in his own house dishes are brought of themselves to him (H.I. xxxii). He makes spectres appear in the market place; when he walks out statues move, and shadows go before him which he says are souls of the dead (H. IV. iv).

On one occasion Aquila says he was present when Luna was seen looking out of all the windows of a tower on all sides at once (R. II. xi).

The most peculiar incident, however, is the use Simon is said to have made of the soul of a dead boy, by which he did many of his wonders. The incident is found in both accounts, but more fully in the *Homilies* (I. xxv-xxx) than in the *Recognitions* (II. xiii-xv), for which reason the text of the former is followed.

Simon did not stop at murder, as he confessed to Nicetas and Aquila "as a friend to friends." In fact he separated the soul of a boy from his body to act as a confederate in his phenomena. And this is the magical *modus operandi*. "He delineates the boy on a statue which he keeps consecrated in the inner part of the house where he sleeps, and he says that after he has fashioned him out of the air by certain divine transmutations, and has sketched his form, he returns him again to the air."

Simon explains the theory of this practice as follows:

"First of all the spirit of the man having been turned into the nature of heat draws in and absorbs, like a cupping-glass, the surrounding air; next he turns the air which comes within the envelope of spirit into water. And the air in it not being able to escape owing to the confining force of the spirit, he changed it into the nature of blood, and the blood solidifying made flesh; and so when the flesh is solidified he exhibited a man made of air and not of earth. And thus having persuaded himself of his ability to make a new man of air, he reversed the transmutations, he said, and returned him to the air."

When the converts thought that this was the soul of the person, Simon laughed and said, that in the phenomena it was not the soul, "but some daemon[69] who pretended to be the soul that took possession of people."

The coming controversy with Simon is then explained by Peter to Clement to rest on certain passages of scripture. Peter admits that there are falsehoods in the scriptures, but says that it would never do to explain this to the people. These falsehoods have been permitted for certain righteous reasons (H. III. v).

"For the scriptures declare all manner of things that no one of those who enquire unthankfully may discover the truth, but (simply) what he wishes to find" (H. III. x).

In the lengthy explanation which follows, however, on the passages Simon is going to bring forward, such as the mention of a plurality of gods, and God's hardening men's hearts, Peter states that in reality all the passages which speak against God are spurious additions, but this is to be guarded as an esoteric secret.

Nevertheless in the public controversy which follows, this secret is made public property, in order to meet Simon's declaration: "I say that there are many gods, but one God of all these gods, incomprehensible and unknown to all" (R. II. xxxviii); and again: "My belief is that there is a Power of immeasurable and ineffable Light, whose greatness is held to be incomprehensible, a power which the maker of the world even does not know, nor does Moses the lawgiver, nor your master Jesus" (R. II. xlix).

A point of interest to be noticed is that Peter challenges Simon to substantiate his statements by quotations either from the scriptures of the Jews, or from some they had not heard of, or from those of the Greeks, or from *his own* scriptures (R. II. xxxviii).

Simon argues that finding the God of the Law imperfect, he concludes this is not the supreme God. After a wordy harangue of Peter, Simon is said to have been worsted by Peter's threatening to go to Simon's bed-chamber and question the soul of the murdered boy. Simon flies to Tyre (H.) or Tripolis (R.), and Peter determines to pursue him among the Gentiles.

The two accounts here become exceedingly contradictory and confused. According to the *Homilies*, Simon flees from Tyre to Tripolis, and thence further to Syria. The main dispute takes place at Laodicæa on the unity of God (XVI. i). Simon appeals to the *Old Testament* to show that there are many gods (XVI. iv); shows that the scriptures contradict themselves (XVI. ix); accuses Peter of using magic and teaching doctrines different to those taught by Christ (XVII. ii-iv); asserts that Jesus is not consistent with himself (XVII. v); that the maker of the world is not the highest God (XVIII. i); and declares the Ineffable Deity (XVIII. iv).[70] Peter of course refutes him (XVIII. xii-xiv), and Simon retires.

The last incident of interest takes place at Antioch. Simon stirs up the people against Peter by representing him as an impostor. Friends of Peter set the authorities on Simon's track, and he has to flee. At Laodicæa he meets Faustinianus (R.), or Faustus (H.), the father of Clement, who rebukes him (H. XIX. xxiv); and so he changes the face of Faustinianus into an exact likeness of his own that he may be taken in his place (H. XX. xii; R.X. liii). Peter sends the transformed Faustinianus to Antioch, who, in the guise of Simon, makes a confession of imposture and testifies to the divine mission of Peter. Peter accordingly enters Antioch in triumph.

The story of Simon in the *Apostolic Constitutions* is short and taken from the *Acts*, and to some extent from the Clementines, finishing up, however, with the mythical death of Simon at Rome, owing to the prayers of Peter. Simon is here said to be conducted by daemons and to have flown (uπτατο) upwards. The details of this magical feat are given variously elsewhere.[71]

The only point of real interest is a vague reference to Simonian literature (VI. xvi), in a passage which runs as follows:

For we know that the followers of Simon and Cleobius having composed poisonous books in the name of Christ and his disciples, carry them about for the deception of you who have loved Christ and us his servants.[72]

So end the most important of the legends. To these, however, must be added others of a like nature of which the scene of action is laid at Rome in the time of Nero.[73] I have not thought it worth while to refer to the original texts for these utterly apocryphal and unauthenticated stories, but simply append a very short digest from the excellent summary of Dr. Salmon, the Regius Professor of Divinity in Dublin University, as given in Smith and Wace's *Dictionary of Christian Biography*.[74]

The Greek *Acts of Peter and Paul* give details of the conflict and represent both apostles as having taken part in it. Simon and Peter are each required to raise a dead body to life. Simon, by his magic, makes the head move, but as soon as he leaves the body it again becomes lifeless. Peter, however, by his prayers effects a real resurrection. Both are challenged to divine what the other is planning. Peter prepares blessed bread, and takes the emperor into the secret.

Simon cannot guess what Peter has been doing, and so raises hell-hounds who rush on Peter, but the presentation of the blessed bread causes them to vanish.

In the *Acts of Nereus and Achilleus*,[75] another version of the story is given. Simon had fastened a great dog at his door in order to prevent Peter entering. Peter by making the sign of the cross renders the dog tame towards himself, but so furious against his master Simon that the latter had to leave the city in disgrace.

Simon, however, still retains the emperor's favour by his magic power. He pretends to permit his head to be cut off, and by the power of glamour appears to be decapitated, while the executioner really cuts off the head of a ram.

The last act of the drama is the erection of a wooden tower in the Campus Martius, and Simon is to ascend to heaven in a chariot of fire. But, through the prayers of Peter, the two daemons who were carrying him aloft let go their hold and so Simon perishes miserably.

Dr. Salmon connects this with the story, told by Suetonius[76] and Dio Chrysostom,[77] that Nero caused a wooden theatre to be erected in the Campus, and that a gymnast who tried to play the part of Icarus fell so near the emperor as to bespatter him with blood.

So much for these motley stories; here and there instructive, but mostly absurd. I shall now endeavour to sift out the rubbish from this patristic and legendary heap, and perhaps we shall find more of value than at present appears.

NOTES:

[1]

Smith's *Dictionary of the Bible*, art. "Acts of the Apostles."

[2]

Ibid.

[3]

Lit. powers.

[4]

The Romans.

[5]

Claudius was the fourth of the Cæsars, and reigned from A.D. 41-54.

[6]

Lit., stood on a roof; an Eastern metaphor.

[7]

The technical term for this transmigration, used by Pythagoreans and others, is μεταγγισμος, the pouring of water from one vessel (αγγος) into another.

[8]

This famous lyric poet, whose name was Tisias, and honorific title Stesichorus, was born about the middle of the seventh century B.C., in Sicily. The story of his being deprived of sight by Castor and Pollux for defaming their sister Helen is mentioned by many classical writers. The most familiar quotation is the Horatian (*Ep.* xvii. 42-44):

> Infamis Helenæ Castor offensus vicem
> Fraterque magni Castoris victi prece.
> Adempta vati redidere lumina.

[9]

That is to say, the heretics.

[10]

In a preceding part of the book against the "Magicians."

[11]

Deuteronomy, iv. 24.

[12]

Heracleitus of Ephesus flourished about the end of the sixth century B.C. He was named the obscure from the difficulty of his writings.

[13]

I put the few direct quotations we have from Simon in italics.

[14]

Isaiah, v. 7.

[15]

I Peter, i. 24.

[16]

Empedocles of Agrigentum, in Sicily, flourished about B.C. 444.

[17]

φρονησις, consciousness?

[18]

Syzygies.

[19]

Isaiah, i. 2.

[20]

I Corinth., xi. 32.

[21]

το μηκετι γινομενον.

[22]

See *Jeremiah*, i. 5.

[23]

Genesis, ii, 10.

[24]

Veins and arteries are said not to have been distinguished by ancient physiologists.

[25]

A lacuna unfortunately occurs here in the text. The missing words probably identified "that which is commonly called by everyone the navel" with the umbilical cord.

[26]

This is omitted by Miller in the first Oxford edition.

[27]

Odyssey, x. 304, *seqq.*

[28]

λογος.

[29]

Cf. *Isaiah,* ii. 4.

[30]

Cf. *Luke,* iii. 9.

[31]

Or adorning.

[32]

Genesis, iii. 24.

[33]

λογος; also reason.

[34]

αντιστοιχοντες; used in Xenophon (*Ana.* v. 4, 12) of two bands of dancers facing each other in rows or pairs.

[35]

He who has stood, stands and will stand.

[36]

Thought.

[37]

The Middle Distance.

[38]

There is a lacuna in the text here.

[39]

δια της ιδιας επιγνωσεως.

[40]

Undergo the passion.

[41]

παρεδρους C.W. King calls these "Assessors." (*The Gnostics and their Remains*, p. 70.)

[42]

This is presumably meant for a grim patristic joke.

[43]

A medicinal drug used by the ancients, especially as a specific against madness.

[44]

The conducting of souls to or from the invisible world.

[45]

προυνικος: προυνεικς is one who bears burdens, a carrier; in a bad sense it means lewd.

[46]

Or the conception (of the mind).

[47]

Cf. 1 *Thess.*, v. 8.

[48]

A famous actor and mime writer who flourished in the time of Augustus (circa A.D. 7); there are extant some doubtful fragments of Philistion containing moral sentiments from the comic poets.

[49]

πληρωμα

[50]

Scripture.

[51]

Matth., v. 17.

[52]

John, v. 46, 47.

[53]

Matth., xix. 10-12.

[54]

Matth., xix. 6.

[55]

αρχη the same word is translated "dominion" when applied to the aeons of Simon.

[56]

Genesis, i. 1.

[57]

Matth., xi. 25.

[58]

"The all-evil Daemon, the avenger of men," of the Prologue.

[59]

Mythologies.

[60]

"Rootage," rather, to coin a word. ριζωμα must be distinguished from ριζα, a root, the word used a few sentences later.

[61]

Dictionary of Christian Biography (Ed. Smith and Wace), art. "Clementine Literature," I. 575.

[62]

Dictionary of Sects, Heresies, etc. (Ed. Blunt), art. "Ebionites."

[63]

The two accounts are combined in the following digest, and in the references H. stands for the *Homiles* and R. for the *Recognitions*.

[64]

Some twenty-three miles.

[65]

We have little information of the Hemero-baptists, or Day-baptists. They are said to have been a sect of the Jews and to have been so called for daily performing certain ceremonial ablutions (Epiph., *Contra Hær.*, I. 17). It is conjectured that they were a sect of the Pharisees who agreed with the Sadducees in denying the resurrection. *The Apostolic Constitutions* (VI. vii) tell us of the Hemero-baptists, that "unless they wash themselves every day they do not eat, nor will they use a bed, dish, bowl, cup, or seat, unless they have purified it with water."

[66]

κατα τον της συζυγιας λογον.

[67]

This has led to the conjecture that the translation was made from the false reading Selene instead of Helene, while Bauer has used it to support his theory that Justin and those who have followed him confused the Phoenician worship of solar and lunar divinities of similar names with the worship of Simon and Helen.

[68]

This is not to be confused with the Dositheus of Origen, who claimed to be a Christ, says Matter (*Histoire Critique du Gnosticisme*, Tom. i. p. 218, n. 1st. ed., 1828).

[69]

An elemental.

[70]

πατηρ εν απορρητοις.

[71]

Hegesippus (*De Bello Judaico*, iii. 2), Abdias (*Hist.*, i, towards the end), and Maximus Taurinensis (*Patr. VI. Synodi ad Imp. Constant.*, Act. 18), say that Simon flew like Icarus; whereas in Arnobius (*Contra Gentes*, ii) and the Arabic Preface to Council of Nicæa there is talk of a chariot of fire, or a car that he had constructed.

[72]

Cotelerius in a note (i. 347, 348) refers the reader to the passages in the *Recognitions* and in Jerome's *Commentary on Matthew,* which I have already quoted. He also says that the author of the book, *De Divinis Nominibus* (C. 6), speaks of "the controversial sentences of Simon" (Σιμωνος αντιρρητικοι λογοι). The author is the Pseudo-Dionysius the Areopagite, and I shall quote later on some of these sentences, though from a very uncertain source. Cotelerius also refers to the Arabic Preface to the Nicaean Council. The text referred to will be found in the Latin translation of Abrahamus Echellensis, given in Labbé's *Concilia (Sacrorum Conciliorum Nova Collectio,* edd. Phil. Labbæus et Gabr. Cossartius, S.J., Florentiæ, 1759, Tom. ii, p. 1057, col. 1), and runs as follows:

"Those traitors (the Simonians) fabricated for themselves a gospel, which they divided into four books, and called it the 'Book of the Four Angles and Points of the World.' All pursue magic zealously, and defend it, wearing red and rose-coloured threads round the neck in sign of a compact and treaty entered into with the devil their seducer."

As to the books of the followers of Cleobius we have no further information.

[73]

A.D. 54-68.

[74]

Art. "Simon Magus," Vol. IV. p. 686.

[75]

Bolland, *Acta SS.* May iii. 9.

[76]

vi. 12.

[77]

Orat. xxi. 9.

PART II.

A REVIEW OF AUTHORITIES.

The student will at once perceive that though the Simon of the *Acts* and the Simon of the fathers both retain the two features of the possession of magical power and of collision with Peter, the tone of the narratives is entirely different. Though the apostles are naturally shown as rejecting with indignation the pecuniary offer of the thaumaturge, they display no hate for his personality, whereas the fathers depict him as the vilest of impostors and charlatans and hold him up to universal execration. The incident of Simon's offering money to Peter is admittedly taken by the fathers from this account, and therefore their repetition in no way corroborates the story. Hence its authenticity rests entirely with the writer of the *Acts*, for Justin, who was a native of Samaria, does not mention it. As the *Acts* are not quoted from prior to A.D. 177, and their writer is only traditionally claimed to be Luke, we may safely consider ourselves in the domain of legend and not of history.

The same may be said of all the incidents of Simon's career; they pertain to the region of fable and probably owe their creation to the Patristic and Simonian controversies of later ages.

The Simon of Justin gives us the birthplace of Simon as at Gitta, and the rest of the fathers follow suit with variation of the name. Gitta, Gittha, Gittoi, Gitthoi, Gitto, Gitton, Gitteh, so run the variants. This, however, is a matter of no great importance, and the little burg is said to-day to be called Gitthoï.[78]

The statement of Justin as to the statue of Simon at Rome with the inscription "SIMONI DEO SANCTO" has been called in question by every scholar since the discovery in 1574 of a large marble fragment in the island of the Tiber bearing the inscription "SEMONI SANCO DEO FIDIO," a Sabine God. A few, however, think that Justin could not have made so glaring a mistake in writing to the Romans, and that if it were a mistake Irenæus would not have copied it. The coincidence, however, is too striking to bear any other interpretation than that perhaps some ignorant controversialist had endeavoured to give the legend a historical appearance, and that Justin had lent a too ready ear to him. It is also to be noticed that Justin tells us that nearly all the Samaritans were Simonians.

We next come to the Simon of Irenæus which, owing to many similarities, is supposed by scholars to have been taken from Justin's account, if not from the *Apology*, at any rate from Justin's lost work on heresies which he speaks of in the *Apology*. Or it may be that both borrowed from some common source now lost to us.

The story of Helen is here for the first time given. Whether or not there was a Helen we shall probably never know. The "lost sheep" was a necessity of every Gnostic system, which taught the descent of the soul into matter. By whatever name called, whether Sophia, Acamôth, Prunîcus, Barbêlo, the glyph of the Magdalene, out of whom seven devils are cast, has yet to be understood, and the mystery of the Christ and the seven aeons, churches or assemblies (*ecclesiæ*), in every man will not be without significance to every student of Theosophy. These data are common to all Gnostic aeonology.

If it is argued that Simon was the first inventor of this aeonology, it is astonishing that his name and that of Helen should not have had some recognition in the succeeding systems. If, on the contrary, it is maintained that he used existing materials for his system, and explained away his improper connection with Helen by an adaptation of the Sophia-mythos, it is difficult to understand how such a palpable absurdity could have gained any credence among such cultured adherents as the Simonians evidently were. In either case the Gnostic tradition is shown to be pre-Christian. Every initiated Gnostic, however, must have known that the mythos referred to the World-Soul in the Cosmos and the Soul in man.

The accounts of the *Acts* and of Justin and Irenæus are so confusing that it has been supposed that two Simons are referred to.[79] For if he claimed to be a reïncarnation of Jesus, appearing in Jerusalem as the Son, he could not have been contemporary with the apostles. It follows, therefore, that either he made no such claim; or if he made the claim, Justin and Irenæus had such vague information that they confused him with the Simon of the *Acts*; or that the supposition is not well-founded, and Simon was simply inculcating the esoteric doctrine of the various manifestations or descents of one and the same Christ principle.

The Simon of Tertullian again is clearly taken from Irenæus, as the critics are agreed. "Tertullian evidently knows no more than he read in Irenæus," says Dr. Salmon.[80]

It is only when we come to the Simon of the *Philosophumena* that we feel on any safe ground. The prior part of it is especially precious on account of the quotations from *The Great Revelation* (η μεγαλη αποφασις) which we hear of from no other source. The author of *Philosophumena*, whoever he was, evidently had access to some of the writings of the Simonians, and here at last we have arrived at any thing of real value in our rubbish heap.

It was not until the year 1842 that Minoides Mynas brought to Paris from Mount Athos, on his return from a commission given him by the French Government, a fourteenth-century MS. in a mutilated condition. This was the MS. of our *Philosophumena* which is supposed to have been the work of Hippolytus. The authorship, however, is still uncertain, as will appear by what will be said about the Simon of Epiphanius and Philaster.

The latter part of the section on Simon in the *Philosophumena* is not so important, and is undoubtedly taken from Irenæus or from the anti-heretical treatise of Justin, or from the source from which both these fathers drew. The account of the death of Simon, however, shows that the author was not Hippolytus from whose lost work Epiphanius and Philaster are proved by Lipsius to have taken their accounts.

The Simon of Origen gives us no new information, except as to the small number of the Simonians. But like other data in his controversial writings against the Gnostic philosopher Celsus we can place little reliance on his statement, for Eusebius Pamphyli writing in A.D. 324-5, a century afterwards, speaks of the Simonians as still considerable in numbers.[81]

The Simon of Epiphanius and Philaster leads us to speak of a remarkable feat of scholarship performed by R.A. Lipsius,[82] the learned professor of divinity in the university of Jena. From their accounts he has reconstructed to some extent a lost work of Hippolytus against heresies of which a description was given by Photius. This treatise was founded on certain discourses of Irenæus. By comparing Philaster, Epiphanius, and the Pseudo-Tertullian, he recovers Hippolytus, and by comparing his restored Hippolytus with Irenæus he infers a common authority, probably the lost work of Justin Martyr, or, may we suggest, as remarked above, the work from which Justin got his information.[83]

The Simon of Theodoret differs from that of his predecessor only in one or two important details of the aeonology, a fact that has presumably led Matter to suppose that he has introduced some later Gnostic ideas or confused the teachings of the later Simonians with those of Simon.[84]

The Simon of the legends is so entirely outside any historical criticism, and the stories gleaned from the *Homilies* and *Recognitions* are so evidently fabrications—most probably added to the doctrinal narrative at a later date—and so obviously the stock-in-trade legends of magic, that not a solitary scholar supports their authenticity. Probably one of the reasons for this is the strong Ebionism of the narratives, which is by no means palatable to the orthodox taste. In this connection the following table of the Ebionite scheme of emanation may be of interest:

GOD.
(The One Being, The principles of all things.)

SPIRIT.	MATTER The Four elements. (This mixture produces)
THE SON. (The Leader of the future cycle.)	THE DEVIL. (The leader of the present cycle.)
GREAT THINGS. (Heaven, light, life, etc.)	LITTLE THINGS. (Earth, fire, death, etc.)
ADAM. (Truth.)	EVE. (Error.)

MAN.

(The Union of Spirit and Body, of Truth and Error.)

INFERIOR MEN.	SUPERIOR MEN.
Ishmael.	Isaac.
Esau.	Jacob.
Aaron.	Moses.
John the Baptist.	Jesus.
Antichrist.	Christ.

GOD.

(Completion, rest.)[85]

There remains but to mention the curious theory of Bauer and the Tubingen school. It is now established by recent theological criticism that the Clementine writings were the work of some member or members of the Elkesaites, a sect of the Ebionites, and that they were written at Rome somewhere in the third century. The Elkessæans or Elkesaites founded their creed on a book called *Elkesai*, which purported to be an angelic revelation and which was remarkable for its hostility to the apostle Paul. As the *Recognitions* contain much anti-Paulinism, Bauer and his school not only pointed out the Ebionite source of the Clementine literature, but also put forward the theory that whenever Simon Magus is mentioned Paul is intended; and that the narrative of the *Acts* and the legends simply tell the tale of the jealousy of the elder apostles to Paul, and their attempt to keep him from the fullest enjoyment of apostolic privileges. But the latest scholarship shakes its head gravely at the theory, and however bitter controversialists the anti-Paulinists may have been, it is not likely that they would have gone so far out of their way to vent their feelings in so grotesque a fashion.

In conclusion of this Part let us take a general review of our authorities with regard to the life of Simon and the immoral practices attributed to his followers, including a few words of notice on the lost Simonian literature, and reserving the explanation of his system and some notice of magical practices for Part III.

I have distinguished the Simon of the fathers from the Simon of the legends, as to biography, "by convention" and not "by nature," as the Simonians would say, for the one and the other is equally on a mythical basis. It is easy to understand that the rejection of the Simon of the legends is a logical necessity for those who have to repudiate the Ebionite Clementines. Admit the authenticity of the narrative as regards Simon, and the authenticity of the other incidents about John the Baptist and Peter would have to be acknowledged; but this would never do, so Simon escapes from the clutches of his orthodox opponents as far as this count is concerned.

But the biographical incidents in the fathers are of a similar nature precisely to those in the Clementines, and their sources of information are so vague and unreliable, and at such a distance from the time of their supposed occurrence, that we have every reason to place them in the same category with the Clementine legends. Therefore, whether we reject the evidence or accept it, we must reject both accounts or accept both. To reject the one and accept the other is a prejudice that a partisan may be guilty of, but a position which no unbiassed enquirer can with justice take up.

The legends, however, may find some excuse when it is remembered that they were current in a period when the metal of religious controversy was glowing at white heat. Orthodox Christians had their ears still tingling with the echoing of countless accusations of the foulest nature to which they had been subjected. Not a crime that was known or could be imagined that had not been brought against them; they naturally, therefore, returned the compliment when they could do so with safety, and though in these more peaceful and tolerant days much as we may regret the flinging backwards and forwards of such vile accusations, we may still find some excuse for it in the passionate enthusiasm of the times, always, however, remembering that the readiest in accusation and in putting the worst construction on the actions of others, is generally one who unconsciously brings a public accusation against his own lower nature.

This has been well noticed by Matter, who writes as follows:

"There is nothing so impure," says Eusebius, "and one cannot imagine anything so criminal, but the sect of the Simonians goes far beyond it."[86]

The bolt of Eusebius is strong; it is even too strong; for one can imagine nothing that goes beyond the excess of criminality; and Eusebius, belonging to a community who were just escaping from punishments into which accusations no less grave had caused them to be dragged, should not perhaps have allowed himself to speak as he does. But man is made thus; he pursues when he ceases to be pursued.[87]

All societies that have secret rites and a public position, as was the case with all the early communities of Christians and Gnostics, have had like accusations brought against them. The communities of the Simonians and Christians may or may not have been impure, it is now impossible to pronounce a positive opinion. The important point to notice is that the accusations being identical and the evidence or want of evidence the same, condemnation or acquittal must be meted out to both; and that if one is condemned and the other acquitted, the judgment will stand condemned as biassed, and therefore be set aside by those who prefer truth to prejudice.

So eager were the fathers to discredit Simon that they contradict themselves in the most flagrant fashion on many important points. On the one hand we hear that Samaria received the seed of the Word from the apostles and Simon in despair had to flee, on the other hand Justin, a native of Samaria, tells us, a century after this supposed event, that nearly all the Samaritans are Simonians. The accounts of Simon's death again are contradictory; if Simon perished so miserably at Rome, it is the reverse of probable that the Romans would have set up a statue in his honour. But, indeed, it is a somewhat thankless task to criticize such manifest inventions; we know the source of their inspiration, and we know the fertility of the religious imagination, especially in matters of controversy, and this is a sufficient sieve wherewith to sift them out of our heap.

I must now say a few words on Simonian literature of which the only geniune specimens we can in any way be certain are the quotations from the *Apophasis* of Simon in the text of the *Philosophumena*.

That there was a body of Simonian scriptures is undoubtedly true, as may be seen from the passages we have quoted from the *Recognitions,* Jerome, Pseudo-Dionysius and the Arabic Preface to the Nicaean Council, and for some time I was in hopes of being able to collect at least some scattered fragments of these works, but they have all unfortunately shared the fate of much else of value that the ignorance and fear of orthodoxy has committed to the flames. We know at any rate that there was a book called *The Four Quarters of the World,* just as the four orthodox gospels are dedicated to the signs of the four quarters in the old MSS., and that a collection of sentences or controversial replies of Simon were also held in repute by Simonians and were highly distasteful to their opponents. Matter[88] and Amélineau[89] speak of a book by the disciples of Simon called *De la Prédication de S. Paul,* but neither from their references nor elsewhere can I find out any further information. In Migne's *Encyclopédie Théologique,*[90] also, a reference is given to M. Miller (*Catalogue des Manuscripts Grecs de l'Escurial,* p. 112), who is said to mention a Greek MS. on the subject of Simon ("un écrit en grec relatif à Simon"). But I cannot find this catalogue in the British Museum, nor can I discover any other mention of this MS. in any other author.

At last I thought that I had discovered something of real value in Grabe's *Spicilegium,* purporting to be gleanings of fragments from the heretics of the first three centuries A.D.,[91] but the date of the authority is too late to be of much value. Grabe refers to the unsatisfactory references I have already given and, to show the nature of these books, according to the opinion of the unknown author or authors of the *Apostolic Constitutions* (Grabe calls him the "collector," and for some reason best known to himself places him in the fourth century[92]), quotes the following passage from their legendary pages.

"Such were the doings of these people with names of ill-omen slandering the creation and marriage, providence, child-bearing, the Law and the Prophets; setting down foreign names of Angels, as indeed they themselves say, but in reality, of Daemons, who answer back to them from below."

It is only when Grabe refers to the Simonian *Antirrhêtikoi Logoi*, mentioned by the Pseudo-Dionysius, which he calls "vesani Simonis Refutatorii Sermones," that we get any new information.

A certain Syrian bishop, Moses Barcephas, writing in the tenth century,[93] professes to preserve some of these controversial retorts of Simon, which the pious Grabe—to keep this venom, as he calls it, apart from the orthodox refutation—has printed in italics. The following is the translation of these italicized passages:

"God willed that Adam should not eat of that tree; but he did eat; he, therefore, did not remain as God willed him to remain: it results, therefore, that the maker of Adam was impotent."

"God willed that Adam should remain in Paradise; but he of his own disgraceful act fell from thence: therefore the God that made Adam was impotent, inasmuch as he was unable of his own will to keep him in Paradise."

"(For) he interdicted (he said) Adam from the tree of the knowledge of good and evil, by tasting which he would have had power to judge between good and evil, and to avoid this, and follow after that."

"But (said he) had not that maker of Adam forbidden him to eat of that tree, he would in no way have undergone this judgment and this punishment; for hence is evil here, in that he (Adam) had done contrary to the bidding of God, for God had ordered him not to eat, and he had eaten."

"Through envy (said he) he forbade Adam to taste of the tree of life, so that, of course, he should not be immortal."

"For what reason on earth (said he) did God curse the serpent? For if (he cursed him) as the one who caused the harm, why did he not restrain him from so doing, that is, from seducing Adam? But if (he cursed him) as one who had brought some advantage, in that he was the cause of Adam's eating of that good tree, it needs must follow that he was distinctly unrighteous and envious; lastly, if, although from neither of these reasons, he still cursed him, he (the maker of Adam) should most certainly be accused of ignorance and folly."

Now although there seems no reason why the above contentions should not be considered as in substance the arguments employed by Simon against his antagonists of the dead-letter, yet the tenth century is too late to warrant verbal accuracy, unless there may have been some Syrian translation which escaped the hands of the destroyers. The above quoted specimen of traditionary Simonian logic, however, is interesting, and will, we believe, be found not altogether out of date in our own times.[94]

Finally, there is one further point that I have reserved for the end of this Part in order that my readers may constantly keep it in mind during the perusal of the Part which follows.

We must always remember that every single syllable we possess about Simon comes from the hands of bitter opponents, from men who had no mercy or toleration for the heretic. The heretic was accursed, condemned eternally by the very fact of his heresy; an emissary of Satan and the natural enemy of God. There was no hope for him, no mercy for him; he was irretrievably damned.[95] The Simon of our authorities has no friend; no one to say a word in his favour; he is hounded down the byways of "history" and the highways of tradition, and to crush him is to do God service. One solitary ray of light beams forth in the fragment of his work called *The Great Revelation*, one solitary ray, that will illumine the garbled accounts of his doctrine, and speak to the Theosophists of to-day in no uncertain tones that each may say:

Methinks there is much reason in his sayings. If thou consider rightly of the matter, [Simon] has had great wrong.[96]

NOTES:

[78]

M.E. Amélineau, "Essai sur le Gnosticisme Égyptien," *Annales du Musée Guimet*, Tom. xvi. p. 28.

[79]

Mosheim's *Institutes of Ecclesiastical History* (Trans. etc., Murdock and Soames; ed. Stubbs 1863), Vol. I., p. 87, note, gives the following list of those who have maintained the theory of two Simons: Vitringa, *Observ. Sacrar.*, v. 12, § 9, p. 159, C.A. Heumann, *Acta Erudit.*

Lips. for April, A.D. 1727, p. 179, and Is. de Beausobre, *Diss. sur l'Adamites,* pt. ii. subjoined to L'Enfants' *Histoire de la Guerre des Hussites,* i. 350, etc. Dr. Salmon also holds this theory.

[80]

Dict. Christ. Biog., art. "Helena," Vol. II, p. 880.

[81]

Hist. Eccles., ii. 13.

[82]

Quellenkritik des Epiphanios.

[83]

Cf. Dr. Salmon's art. "Hippolytus Romanus," *Dict. Christ. Biog.*, iii. 93, 94.

[84]

Histoire Critique du Gnosticisme, Tom. i. p. 197 (1st ed. 1828).

[85]

Les Bibles, et les Initiateurs Religieux de l'Humanité, Louis Leblois, i. 144; from Uhlhorn, *Die Homilien und Recognitionen*, p. 224.

[86]

Hist. Eccles., ii. 13.

[87]

Op. cit., i. 213.

[88]

Op. cit., ii. 217.

[89]

Op. cit., 32.

[90]

Tom. xxiii, "Dictionnaire des Apocryphes," Vol. II., Index, pp. lxviii, lxix.

[91]

Spicilegium SS. Patrum ut et Haereticorum Sæculorum post Christum natum, I, II et III; Johannes Ernestus Grabius; Oxoniæ, 1714, ed. alt., Vol. I., pp. 305-312.

[92]

P. 306.

[93]

Comment. de Paradiso, c. i., pp. 200, *et seqq.*, editionis Antverpiensis, anno 1567, in 8vo.

[94]

Grabe is also interesting for a somewhat wild speculation which he quotes from a British Divine (apud Usserium in *Antiquitatibus Eccles. Britannicae*), that the tonsure of the monks was taken from the Simonians. (Grabe, *op. cit.*, p, 697.)

[95]

In the epistle of St. Ignatius *Ad Trallianos* (§ 11), Simon is called "the first-born Son of the Devil" (πρωτοτοκον διαβολου υιον); and St. Polycarp seems to refer to Simon in the following passage in his Epistle *Ad Philipp.* (§ 7):

"Everyone who shall not confess that Jesus Christ has come in the flesh, is antichrist, and who shall not confess the martyrdom of the cross, is of the Devil; and he who translates the words of the Lord according to his own desires, and says there is neither resurrection nor judgment, he is *the first-born of Satan.*"

PART III.

THE THEOSOPHY OF SIMON.

In treating of eschatology and the beginning of things the human mind is ever beset with the same difficulties, and no matter how grand may be the effort of the intellect to transcend itself, the finite must ever fail to comprehend the infinite. How much less then can words define that which even the whole phenomenal universe fails to express! The change from the One to the Many is not to be described. How the All-Deity becomes the primal Trinity, is the eternal problem set for man's solution. No system of religion or philosophy has ever explained this inexplicable mystery, for it cannot be understood by the embodied Soul, whose vision and comprehension are dulled by the grossness of its physical envelope. Even the illuminated Soul that quits its prison house, to bathe in the light of infinitude, can only recollect flashes of the Vision Glorious once it returns again to earth.

And this is also the teaching of Simon when he says:

I say there are many gods, but one God of all these gods, incomprehensible and unknown to all, ... a Power of immeasurable and ineffable Light, whose greatness is held to be incomprehensible, a Tower which the maker of the world does not know.

This is a fundamental dogma of the Gnôsis in all climes and in all ages. The demiurgic deity is not the All-Deity, for there is an infinite succession of universes, each having its particular deity, its Brahmâ, to use the Hindû term, but this Brahmâ is not THAT which is Para-Brahman, that which is beyond Brahmâ.

This view of the Simonian Gnôsis has been magnificently anticipated in the *Rig Veda* (x. 129) which reads in the fine translation of Colebrooke as follows:

That, whence all this great creation came,
Whether Its will created or was mute,
The Most High Seer that is in highest Heaven,
He knows it—or perchance even He knows not.

In treating of emanation, evolution, creation or whatever other term may be given to the process of manifestation, therefore, the teachers deal only with one particular universe; the Unmanifested Root, and Universal Cause of all Universes lying behind, in potentiality (δυναμις), in Incomprehensible Silence (σιγη ακαταληπτος). For on the "Tongue of the Ineffable" are many "Words" (λογοι), each Universe having its own Logos.

Thus then Simon speaks of the Logos of this Universe and calls it Fire πυρ). This is the Universal Principle or Beginning (των ολων αρχη), or Universal Rootage (ριζωμα των ολων). But this Fire is not the fire of earth; it is Divine Light and Life and Mind, the Perfect

Intellectual (το τελειον νοερον). It is the One Power, "generating itself, increasing itself, seeking itself, finding itself, its own mother, its own father, its sister, its spouse: the daughter, son, mother, and father of itself; One, the Universal Root." It is That, "which has neither beginning nor end, existing in oneness." "Producing itself by itself, it manifested to itself its own Thought (επινοια)."

It is quite true that this symbology of Fire is not original with Simon, but there is also no reason to suppose that the Samaritan teacher plagiarized from Heracleitus when we know that the major part of antiquity regarded fire and the sun as the most fitting symbols of Deity. Of the manifested elements, fire was the most potent, and therefore the most fitting symbol that could be selected in manifested nature.

But what was the Fire of Heracleitus, the Obscure (ο σκοτεινος), as Cicero, with the rest of the ancients, called him, because of his difficult style? What was the Universal Principle of the "weeping philosopher," the pessimist who valued so little the estimation of the vulgar (οχλολοιδορος)? It certainly was no common "fire," certainly no puerile concept to be brushed away by the mere hurling of an epithet.

Heracleitus of Ephesus (*flor. c.* 503 B.C.) was a sincerely religious man in the highest sense of the word, a reformer who strongly opposed the degenerate polytheism and idolatry of his age; he insisted on the impermanence of the phenomenal universe, of human affairs, beliefs and opinions, and declared the One Eternal Reality; teaching that the Self of man was a portion of the Divine Intelligence. The object of his enquiry was Wisdom, and he reproached his vain-glorious countrymen of the city of Diana with the words: "Your *knowledge* of many things does not give you *wisdom*."

In his philosophy of nature he declared the One Thing to be Fire, but Fire of a mystical nature, "self-kindled and self-extinguished," the vital quickening power of the universe. It was that Universal Life, by participation in which all things have their being, and apart from which they are unsubstantial and unreal. This is the "Tree of Life" spoken of by Simon.

In this Ocean of Fire or Life—in every point or atom of it—is inherent a longing to manifest itself in various forms, thus giving rise to the perpetual flux and change of the phenomenal world. This Divine Desire, this "love for everything that lives and breathes," is found in many systems, and especially in the Vedic and Phoenician Cosmogony. In the *Rig Veda* (x. 129), it is that Kâma or Desire "which first arose in It (the Unknown Deity)," elsewhere identified with Agni or Fire. In the fragments of Phoenician Cosmogony, recovered from Sanchuniathon, it is called Pothos (ποθος) and Erôs (ερως).

In its pure state, the Living and Rational Fire of Heracleitus resides in the highest conceivable Heaven, whence it descends stage by stage, gradually losing the velocity of its motion and vitality, until it finally reaches the Earth-stage, having previously passed through that of "Water." Thence it returns to its parent source.

In this eternal flux, the only repose was to be found in the harmony that occasionally resulted from one portion of the Fire in its descent meeting another in its ascent. All this took place under Law and Order, and the Soul of man being a portion of the Fire in its pure state, and therefore an exile here on Earth, could only be at rest by cultivating as the highest good, contentment (ευαρεστησις, or acquiescence to the Law.

The author of the *Philosophumena* professes to give us some additional information on this philosopher who "bewailed all things, condemning the ignorance of all that lives, and of all men, in pity for the life of mortals," but the obscure philosopher does not lend himself very easily to the controversial purposes of the patristic writer. Heracleitus called the Universal Principle (των απαντων αρχη) Intellectual Fire (πυρ νοερον), and said that the sphere surrounding us and reaching to the Moon was filled with evil, but beyond the Moon-sphere it was purer.[97]

The sentences that the author quotes from Heracleitus in Book IX, are not only obscure enough in themselves, but are also rendered all the more obscure by the polemical treatment they are subjected to by the patristic writer. Heracleitus makes the ALL inclusive of all Being and Non-Being, all pairs of opposites, "differentiation and non-differentiation, the generable and ingenerable, mortal and immortal, the Logos and Aeon, and the Father and Son," which he calls the "Just God." This ALL is the "Sadasat-Tatparam yat" of the *Bhaga-*

vad Gîtâ, inclusive of Being (Sat), Non-Being (Asat), and That Which transcends them (Tatparam yat).[98]

This Logos plays an important part in the system of the Ephesian sage, who says that they who give ear to the Logos (the Word or Supreme Reason) know that "All is One" (εν παντα ειδεναι). Such an admission he calls, "Reflex Harmony" (παλιντροπος αρμονιη), like unto the Supernal Harmony, which he calls Hidden or Occult, and declares its superiority to the Manifested Harmony. The ignorance and misery of men arise from their not acting according to this Harmony, that is to say, according to (Divine) Nature (κατα φυσιν).

He also declares that the Aeon, the Emanative Deity, is as a child playing at creation, an idea found in both the Hindû and Hermetic Scriptures. In the former the Universe is said to be the sport (Lîlâ) of Vishnu, who is spoken of in one of his incarnations as Lîlâvatâra, descending on earth for his own pleasure, when as Krishna he assumed the shape of man as a pretence (a purely Docetic doctrine), hence called Lîlâ-mânusha-vigraha; while in the latter we learn from a magic papyrus that Thoth (the God of Wisdom) created the world by bursting into "seven peals of laughter." This, of course, typifies the Bliss of the Deity in Emanation or Creation, caused by that Divine Love and Compassion for all that lives and breathes, which is the well-spring of the Supreme Cause of the Universe.

Diving into the Mystery of Being, Heracleitus showed how a thing could be good or evil, and evil or good, at one and the same time, as for instance sea water which preserved and nourished fishes but destroyed men. So also, speaking in his usual paradoxical manner, which can only be understood by a full comprehension of the dual nature of man,—the real divine entity, and the passing and ever-changing manifestation, which so many take for the whole man—he says:

The immortals are mortal, and the mortals immortal, the former living the death of the latter, and the latter dying the life of the former.[99]

Thus all externals are transitory, for "no one has ever been twice on the same stream, for different waters are constantly flowing down," and therefore in following externals we shall err, for nothing is efficient and forcible except through Harmony, and its subjection to the Divine Fire, the central principle of Life.

Such was the Fire of the distinguished Ephesian, and of like nature was the Fire of Simon with its three primordial hypostases, Incorruptible Form (αφταρτος μορφη), Universal Mind (νους των ολων), and Great Thought (επινοια μεγαλη), synthesized as the Universal Logos, He who has stood, stands and will stand (ο εστως, στας, στησομενος).

But before passing on to the aeonology of Simon, a short delay, to enquire more fully into the notions of the Initiated among the ancients as to the nature of Mystic Fire, will not be without advantage.

If Simon was a Samaritan and learned in the esoteric interpretation of scripture, he could not have failed to be acquainted with the Kabalah, perhaps even with the now lost Chaldæan *Book of Numbers*. Among the books of the Kabalah, the *Zohar*, or "Book of Splendour," speaks of the mysterious "Hidden Light," that which Simon calls the Hidden Fire (το κρυπτον), and tells us of the "Mystery of the Three Parts of the Fire, which are One" as follows:

Began Rabbi Sim-on and said: Two verses are written, "That YHVH thy Elohim is a devouring fire, a zealous Ail (El)" (*Deut.*, iv. 24); again it is written, "But you that cleave unto YHVH your Elohim, are alive, every one of you, this day" (*Deut.*, iv. 4). On this verse "That YHVH thy Elohim is a consuming fire," this we said to the companions; That it is a fire which devours fire, and it is a fire which devours itself and consumes itself, because it is a fire which is more mighty than fire, and it has been so confirmed. But, Come, See! Whoever desires to know the wisdom of the Holy Unity should look in that flame arising from a burning coal or a lighted lamp. This flame comes out only when united with another thing. Come, See! In the flame which goes up are two lights: one light is a bright white and one light is united with a dark or blue; the white light is that which is above and ascends in a straight path, and that below is that dark or blue light, and this light below is the throne to the white light and that white light rests upon it, and they unite one to the other so that they are one. And this dark light, or blue colour, which is below, is the precious throne to the white. And this is the mystery of the blue. And this blue dark throne unites itself with another thing to light that from below, and this awakes it to unite with the upper white light, and this blue or dark, sometimes changes its colour, but that white above never changes its colour, it is always white; but that blue changes to these different colours, sometimes to blue or black and sometimes to a red colour, and this unites itself to two sides. It unites to the above, to that white upper light, and unites itself below to the thing which is under it, which is the burning matter, and this burns and consumes always from the matter below. And this devours that matter below, which connects with it and upon which the blue light rests, therefore this eats up all which connects with it from below, because it is the nature of it, that it devour and consume everything which depends on it and is dead matter, and therefore it eats up everything which connects with it below, and this white light which rests upon it never consumes itself and never changes its light, and therefore said Moses; "That YHVH thy Elohim is a consuming fire." Surely He consumes. It devours and consumes every thing which rests under it; and on this he said: "YHVH is thy Elohim" not "our Elohim," because Moses has been in that white light, Above, which neither devours nor consumes. Come, See! It is not His Will to light that blue light that should unite with that white light, only for Israël; because they cleave or connect under Him. And, Come, See! Although the nature of that dark or blue light is, that it shall consume every thing which joins with it below, still Israël cleaves on Him, Below, ... and although you cleave in Him nevertheless you exist, because it is written: "You are all alive this day." And on this white light rests above a Hidden Light which is stronger. Here is the above mystery of that flame which comes out from it, and in it is the Wisdom of the Above.[100]

And if Chaldæa gave the impulse which enshrined the workings of the Cosmos in such graphic symbology as the above, we are not surprised to read in the Chaldæan Oracles (λογια),[101] ascribed to Zoroaster, that "all things are generated from One Fire."[102] And this Fire in its first energizing was intellectual; the first "Creation" was of Mind and not of Works:

For the Fire Beyond, the first, did not shut up its power (δυναμις) into Matter (υλη) by Works, but by Mind, for the fashioner of the Fiery Cosmos is the Mind of Mind.[103]

A striking similarity with the Simonian system, indeed, rendered all the closer by the Oracle which speaks of that:

Which first leaped forth from Mind, enveloping Fire with Fire, binding them together that it might interblend the mother-vortices,[104] while retaining the flower of its own Fire.[105]

This "flower" of Fire and the vorticle idea is further explained by the Oracle which says:

Thence a trailing whirlwind, the flower of shadowy Fire, leaping into the wombs (or hollows) of worlds. For thence it is that all things begin to stretch below their wondrous rays.[106]

Compare this with the teaching of Simon that the "fruit" of the Tree is placed in the Store-house and not cast into the Fire.

In his aeonology, Simon, like other Gnostic teachers, begins with the Word, the Logos, which springs up from the Depths of the Unknown—Invisible, Incomprehensible Silence. It is true that he does not so name the Great Power, He who has stood, stands and will stand; but that which comes forth from Silence is Speech, and the idea is the same whatever the terminology employed may be. Setting aside the Hermetic teachings and those of the later Gnôsis, we find this idea of the Great Silence referred to several times in the fragments of the Chaldæan Oracles. It is called "God-nourished Silence" σιγη θεοθρεμμων), according to whose divine decrees the Mind that energizes before all energies, abides in the Paternal Depth.[107] Again:

This unswerving Deity is called the Silent One by the gods, and is said to consent (lit. sing together) with the Mind, and to be known by the Souls through Mind alone.[108]

Elsewhere the Oracles demonstrate this Power which is prior to the highest Heaven as "Mystic Silence."[109]

The Word, then, issuing from Silence is first a Monad, then a Duad, a Triad and a Hebdomad. For no sooner has differentiation commenced in it, and it passes from the state of Oneness (μονοτης), than the Duadic and Triadic state immediately supervene, arising, so to say, simultaneously in the mind, for the mind cannot rest on Duality, but is forced by a law of its nature to rest only on the joint emanation of the Two. Thus the first natural resting point is the Trinity. The next is the Hebdomad or Septenary, according to the mathematical formula 2^n-1, the sum of *n* things taken 1, 2, 3 ... *n*, at a time. The Trinity being manifested, *n* here =3; and 2^3-1 = 7.

Thus Simon has six Roots and the Seventh Power, seven in all, as the type of the Aeons in the Plerôma. These all proceed from the Fire. In like manner also the Cabeiric deities of Samothrace and Phoenicia were Fire-gods, born of the Fire. Nonnus tells us they were sons of the mysterious Hephaestus (Vulcan),[110] and Eusebius, in his quotations from Sanchuniathon, that they were *seven* in number.[111] The Vedic Agni (Ignis) also, the God of Fire, is called "Seven-tongued" (Sapta-jihva) and "Seven-flamed" (Sapta-jvâla).[112]

In the *Hibbert Lectures* of 1887, Prof. A.H. Sayce gives the following Hymn of Ancient Babylonia to the Fire-god, from *The Cuneiform Inscriptions of Western Asia* (iv. 15):

1. The (bed) of the earth they took for their border, but the god appeared not,

2. from the foundations of the earth he appeared not to make hostility;

3. (to) the heaven below they extended (their path), and to the heaven that is unseen they climbed afar.

4. In the Star(s) of Heaven was not their ministry; in Mazzaroth (the Zodiacal signs) was their office.

5. The Fire-god, the first-born supreme, into heaven they pursued and no father did he know.

6. O Fire-god, supreme on high, the first-born, the mighty, supreme enjoiner of the commands of Anu!

7. The Fire-god enthrones with himself the friend that he loves.

8. He reveals the enmity of those seven.

9. On the work he ponders in his dwelling-place.

10. O Fire-god, how were those seven begotten, how were they nurtured?

11. Those seven in the mountain of the sunset were born;

12. those seven in the mountain of the sunrise grew up.

13. In the hollows of the earth they have their dwelling;

14. on the high places of the earth their names are proclaimed.

15. As for them, in heaven and earth they have no dwelling, hidden is their name.

16. Among the sentient gods they are not known.

17. Their name in heaven and earth exists not.

18. Those seven from the mountain of the sunset gallop forth;

19. those seven in the mountain of the sunrise are bound to rest.

20. In the hollows of the earth they set the foot.

21. On the high places of the earth they lift the neck.

22. They by nought are known; in heaven and in earth is no knowledge of them.[113]

Though I have no intention of contending that Simon obtained his ideas specifically from Vedic, Chaldæan, Babylonian, Zoroastrian, or Phoenician sources, still the identity of ideas and the probability, almost amounting to conviction for the student, that the Initiated of antiquity all drew from the same sources, shows that there was nothing original in the main features of the Simonian system.

This is also confirmed by the statements in Epiphanius and the *Apostolic Constitutions* that the Simonians gave "barbarous" or "foreign names" to their Aeons. That is to say, names that were neither Greek nor Hebrew. None of these names are mentioned by the Fathers, and probably the Greek terms given by the author of the *Philosophumena* and Theodoret are exoteric equivalents of the mystery names. There is abundant evidence, from gems, monuments and fragments, to show that there was a mystery language employed by the Gnostic and other schools. What this language was no scholar has yet been able to tell us, and it is sufficiently evident that the efforts at decipherment are so far abortive. The fullest and most precious examples of these names and of this language are to be found in the papyri brought back by Bruce from Abyssinia at the latter end of the last century.[114]

Jamblichus tells us that the language of the Mysteries was that of ancient Egypt and Assyria, which he calls "sacred nations," as follows:

But, you ask, why among our symbolical terms (σγμαντικα) we prefer barbarous (words) to our respective native (tongues)? There is also for this a mystic reason. For it was the gods who taught the sacred nations, such as the Egyptians and Assyrians, the whole of their sacred dialect, wherefore we think that we ought to make our own dialects resemble the speech cognate with the gods. Since also the first mode of speech in antiquity was of such a nature, and especially since they who learnt the first names concerning the gods, mingled them with their own tongue—as being suited to such (names) and conformable to them—and handed them down to us, we therefore keep unchanged the rule of this immemorial tradition to our own times. For of all things that are suited to the gods the most akin is manifestly that which is eternal and immutable.[115]

The existence of this sacred tongue perhaps accounts for the constant distinction made by Homer between the language of the gods and that of men.[116] Diodorus Siculus also asserts that the Samothracians used a very ancient and peculiar dialect in their sacred rites.[117]

These "barbarous names" were regarded as of the greatest efficacy and sanctity, and it was unlawful to change them. As the Chaldæan Logia say:

Change not the barbarous names, for in all the nations are there names given by the gods, possessing unspeakable power in the Mysteries.[118]

And the scholiast[119] adds that they should not be translated into Greek.

It is, therefore, most probable that Simon used the one, three, five, and seven syllabled or vowelled names, and that the Greek terms were substitutes that completely veiled the esoteric meaning from the uninitiated.

The names of the seven Aeons, as given by the author of the *Philosophumena*, are as follows: The Image from the Incorruptible Form, alone ordering all things (εικων εξ αφθαρτου μορφης κοσμουσα μονη παντα), also called The Spirit moving on the Waters (το πνευμα το επιφερουμενον επανω του υδατος) and The Seventh Power (η εβδομη δυναμις); Mind (νους) and Thought (επινοια), also called Heaven (ουρανος) and Earth (γη); Voice (φονη) and Name (ονομα),[120] also called Sun (ηλιος) and Moon (σεληνη); Reason (λογισμος) and Reflection (ενθυμησις), also called Air (αηρ) and Water (υδορ).

The first three of these are sufficiently explained in the fragment of Simon's *Great Revelation*, preserved in the *Philosophumena*, and become entirely comprehensible to the student of the Kabalah who is learned in the emanations of the Sephirothal Tree. Mind and Thought are evidently Chokmah and Binah, and the three and seven Sephiroth are to be clearly recognized in the scheme of the Simonian System which is to follow.

Of the two lower Syzygies, or Lower Quaternary of the Aeons, we have no details from the Fathers. We may, however, see some reason for the exoteric names—Voice and Name, Reason and Reflection—from the following considerations:

(1) We should bear in mind what has already been said about the Logos, Speech and Divine Names. (2) In the Septenary the Quaternary represents the Manifested and the Triad the Concealed Side of the Fire. (3) The fundamental characteristics of the manifested universe with the Hindûs and Buddhists are Name (Nâma) and Form (Rûpa). (4) Simon says that the Great Power was not called Father until Thought (in manifestation becoming Voice) *named* (ονομασαι) him Father. (5) Reason and Reflection are evidently the two lowest aspects, principles, or characteristics, of the *divine* Mind of man. These are included in the lower mind, or Internal Organ (Antahkarana), by the Vedântin philosophers of India and called Buddhi and Manas, being respectively the mental faculties used in the certainty of judgment and the doubt of enquiry.

This Quaternary, among a host of other things, typifies the four lower planes, elements, principles, aspects, etc., of the Universe, with their Hierarchies of Angels, Archangels, Rulers, etc., each synthesized by a Lord who is supreme in his own domain. Seeing, however, that the outermost physical plane is so vast that it transcends the power of conception of even the greatest intellect, it is useless for us to speculate on the interplay of cosmic forces and the mysterious interaction of Spheres of Being that transcend all normal human consciousness. It is only on the lowest and outermost plane that the lower Quaternary symbolizes the four Cardinal Points. The Michael (Sun), Gabriel (Moon), Uriel (Venus), and Raphael (Mercury) of the Kabalah, the four Beasts, the Wheels of Ezekiel, were living, divine, and intelligent Entities pertaining to the inner nature of man and the universe for the Initiated.

It is to be presumed that the Simonians had distinct teachings on this point, as is evidenced by the title of their lost work, *The Book of the Four Angles and Points of the World*. The Four Angles were probably connected with the four ducts or Streams of the "River going forth from Eden to water the Garden." These Streams have their analogy on all planes, and cosmically are of the same nature as the Âkâsha-Gangâ—the Ganges in the Akâshic Ocean of Space—and the rest of the Rivers in the Paurânic writings of the Hindûs.

But before going further it will be as well to have a Diagram or Scheme of the Simonian Aeonology, for presumably the School of Simon had such a Scheme, as we know the Ophites had from the work of Origen, *Contra Celsum*.

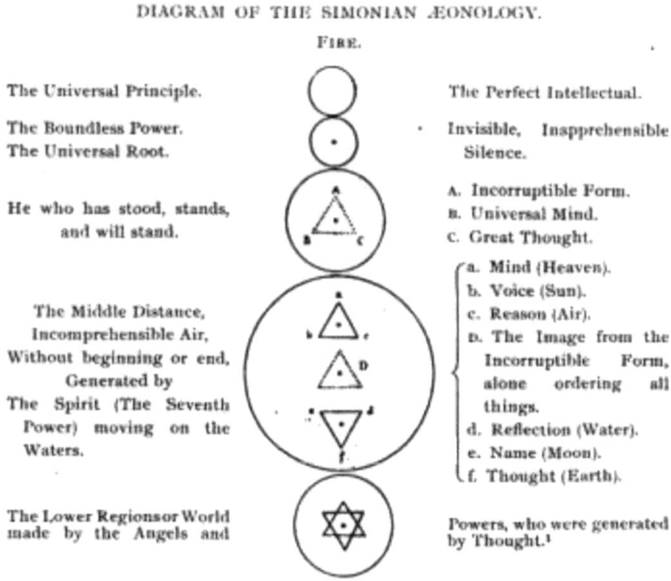

DIAGRAM OF THE SIMONIAN AEONOLOGY.[121]

Of course no Diagram is anything more than a symbolical mnemonic, so to say; in itself it is entirely insufficient and only permits a glance at one aspect, or face, of the world-process. It is a step in a ladder merely, useful only for mounting and to be left aside when once a higher rung is reached. Thus it is that the whole of the elements of Euclid were merely an introduction to the comprehension of the "Platonic Solids," which must also, in their turn, be discarded when the within or essence of things has to be dealt with and not the without or appearance, no matter how "typical" that appearance may be.

Sufficient has already been said of the Universal Principle, of the Universal Root and of the Boundless Power—the Parabrahman (That Which transcends Brahmâ), Mûla-Prakriti (Root-Nature), and Supreme Îshvara, or the Unmanifested Eternal Logos, of the Vedântic Philosophers. The next stage is the potential unmanifested type of the Trinity, the Three in One and One in Three, the Potentialities of Vishnu, Brahmâ, and Shiva, the Preservative, Emanative, and Regenerative Powers—the Supreme Logos, Universal Ideation and Potential Wisdom, called by Simon the Incorruptible Form, Universal Mind and Great Thought. This Incorruptible Form is the Paradigm of all Forms, called Vishva Rûpam or All-Form and the Param Rûpam or Supreme Form, in the *Bhagavad Gîtâ*[122] spoken also of as the Param Nidhânam or Supreme Treasure-house,[123] which Simon also calls the Treasure-house θησαυρος and Storehouse αποθηκη, an idea found in many systems, and most elaborately in that of the *Pistis-Sophia*.

Between this Divine World, the Unmanifested Triple Aeon, and the World of Men is the Middle Distance—the Waters of Space differentiated by the Image or Reflection of the Triple Logos (D) brooding upon them. As there are three Worlds, the Divine, Middle, and Lower, which have been well named by the Valentinians the Pneumatic (or Spiritual), Psychic (or Soul-World), and Hylic (or Material), so in the Middle Distance we have three planes or degrees, or even seven. This Middle Distance contains the Invisible Spheres between the Physical World and the Divine. To it the Initiated and Illuminati, the Spiritual Teachers of all ages, have devoted much exposition and explanation. It is divine and infernal at one and the same time, for as the higher parts—to use a phrase that is clumsy and misleading, but which cannot be avoided—are pure and spiritual, so the lower parts are corrupted and tainted. The law of analogy, imaging and reflection, hold good in every department of emanative nature, and though pure and spiritual ideas come to men from this realm of the Middle Distance, it also receives back from man the impressions of his impure thoughts and desires, so that its lower parts are fouler even than the physical world, for man's secret thoughts and passions are fouler than the deeds he performs. Thus there is a Heaven and Hell in the Middle Distance, a Pneumatic and Hylic state.

The Lord of this Middle World is One in his own Aeon, but in reality a reflection of the triple radiance from the Unmanifested Logos. This Lord is the Manifested Logos, the Spirit moving on the Waters. Therefore all its emanations or creations are triple. The triple Light above and the triple Darkness below, force and matter, or spirit and matter, both owing their being and apparent opposition to the Mind, "alone ordering all things."

The Diagram to be more comprehensible should be so arranged, mentally, that each of the higher spheres is found within or interpenetrating the lower. Thus, from this point of view, the centre is a more important position than above or below. External to all is the Physical Universe, made by the Hylic Angels, that is to say those emanated by Thought, Epinoia, as representing Primeval Mother Earth, or Matter; not the Earth we know, but the Adamic Earth of the Philosophers, the Potencies of Matter, which Eugenius Philalethes assures us, on his honour, no man has ever seen. This Earth is, in one sense, the Protyle for which the most advanced of our modern Chemists are searching as the One Mother Element.

The idea of the Spirit of God moving on the Waters is a very beautiful one, and we find it worked out in much detail in the Hindû scriptures. For instance, in the *Vishnu Purâna*,[124] we find a description of the emanation of the present Universe by the Supreme Spirit, at the beginning of the present Kalpa or Aeon, an infinity of Kalpas and Universes stretching behind. This he creates endowed with the Quality of Goodness, or the Pneumatic Potency. For the three Qualities (or Gunas) of Nature (Prakriti) are the Pneumatic, Psychic and Hylic Potencies of the Waters of Simon.

At the close of the past (or Pâdma) Kalpa, the divine Brahmâ, endowed with the quality of goodness, awoke from his night of sleep, and beheld the universe void. He, the supreme Nârâyana, the incomprehensible, the sovereign of all creatures, invested with the form of Brahmâ, the god without beginning, the creator of all things; of whom, with respect to his name Nârâyana, the god who has the form of Brahmâ, the imperishable origin[125] of the world, this verse is repeated: "The waters are called Nârâ, because they were the offspring of Nara (the supreme spirit); and, as, in them, his first (Ayana)[126] progress (in the character of Brahmâ) took place, he is thence named Nârâyana (he whose place of moving was the waters)."

Sir Wm. Jones translates this well-known verse of Manu[127] as follows:

The waters are called Nârâh, because they were the production of Nara, or the spirit of God; and, since they were his first Ayana, or place of motion, he thence is named Nârâyana or moving on the waters.

Substantially the same statement is made in the *Linga, Vâyu*, and *Mârkandeya Purânas*, and the *Bhâgavata* explains it more fully as follows:

Purusha (the Spirit) having divided the egg (the ideal universe in germ), on his issuing forth in the beginning, desiring a place of motion (Ayanam) for himself, pure he created the waters pure.

In the *Vishnu Purâna*, again, Brahmâ, speaking to the Celestials, says:

I, Mahâdeva (Shiva), and you all are but Nârâyana.[128]

The beautiful symbol of the Divine Spirit moving and brooding over the Primordial Waters of Space—Waters which as differentiation proceeds become more and more turbid—is too graphic to require further explanation. It is too hallowed by age and sanctified by the consent of humanity to meet with less than our highest admiration.

Dissertation on our Diagram could be pursued to almost any length, but sufficient has already been said to show the points of correspondence between the ideas ascribed to Simon and universal Theosophy.

Let us now enquire into the part played by Epinoia, the Divine Thought, in the cosmic process, reserving the part played by her in the human drama to when we come to treat of the soteriology of Simon. We have evidently here a version of the great Sophia-mythus, which plays so important a part in all Gnostic systems. On the one hand the energizings of the mother-side of Divine Nature, on the other the history of the evolution of the Divine Monad, shut into all forms throughout the elemental spheres, throughout the lower kingdoms, up to the man stage.

The mystery of Sophia-Epinoia is great indeed, insoluble in its origins; for how does that which is Divine descend below and create Powers which imprison their parent? It is the mystery of the universe and of man, insoluble for all but the Logos itself, by whose self-sacrifice Sophia, the Soul, is finally freed from her bonds.

Epinoia is a Power of many names. She is called the Mother, or All-Mother, Mother of the Living or Shining Mother, the Celestial Eve; the Power Above; the Holy Spirit, for the Spiritus in some systems is a feminine power (in a symbolical sense, of course), preeminently in the *Codex Nazaræus*, the scripture of the Mandaïtes. Again she is called She of the Left-hand, as opposed to the Christos, He of the Right-hand; the Man-woman; Prouneikos; Matrix; Paradise; Eden; Achamôth; the Virgin; Barbelo; Daughter of Light; Merciful Mother; Consort of the Masculine One; Revelant of the Perfect Mysteries; Perfect Mercy; Revelant of the Mysteries of the Whole Magnitude; Hidden Mother; She who knows the Mysteries of the Elect; the Holy Dove, who has given birth to the two Twins; Ennoia; and by many another name varying according to the terminology of the different systems, but ever preserving the root idea of the World-Soul in the Macrocosm and the Soul in Man.

Within every form, aye, even apparently the meanest, is Epinoia confined; for everything within is innate with Life; every form contains a spark of the Divine Fire, essentially of the same nature as the All; for in the Roots, and also in all things—since all is built on their type—is "the whole of the Boundless Power together *in potentiality*, but not *in actuality*."

The reason given for this imprisonment of Sophia in most of the systems is that she endeavoured to create without her Syzygy, the Father or Nous, wishing to imitate alone the self-generating power of the Supreme. Thus through ignorance she involved herself in suffering, from which she was freed by repentance and experience. What explanation of this supreme mystery was publicly ventured on by Simon we cannot know, for the patristic accounts are confused and contradictory.

Irenæus tells us that:

She was the first Conception (Epinoia) of his Mind, the Mother of All, by whom in the beginning he conceived in his Mind, the making of the Angels and Archangels.

This Epinoia, leaping forth from *him* (the Boundless Power), and knowing what was the will of her Father, descended to the Lower Regions and generated the Angels and Powers, by whom also he said the world was made. And after she had generated them, she was detained by them through envy, for they did not wish to be thought the progeny of another. As for himself he was entirely unknown by them; and it was his Thought (Epinoia) that was made prisoner by the Powers and Angels that had been emanated by her. And she suffered every kind of indignity at their hands to prevent her reäscending to her Father, even to being imprisoned in the human body and transmigrating into other female bodies, as from one vessel into another.

Tertullian's account differs by the important addition that the "design of the Father was prevented"; how or why he does not say.

She was his first Suggestion whereby he suggested the making of the Angels and Archangels; that she sharing in this design had sprung forth from the Father, and leaped down into the Lower Regions; and that there, the design of the Father being prevented, she had brought forth Angelic Powers ignorant of the Father, the artificer of this world (?); by these she was detained, not according to his intention, lest when she had gone they should be thought to be the progeny of another, etc.

The *Philosophumena* say nothing on this point, except that Epinoia "throws all the Powers in the World into confusion through her unsurpassable Beauty."

Philaster renders confusion worse confounded, by writing:

And he also dared to say that the World had been made by Angels, and the Angels again had been made by certain endowed with perception from Heaven, and that they (the Angels) had deceived the human race.

He asserted, moreover, that there was a certain other Thought (Intellectus) who descended into the world for the salvation of men.

Epiphanius further complicates the problem as follows:

This Power (Prunîcus and Holy Spirit) descending from Above changed its form.... And through the Power from Above ... displaying her beauty, she drove them to frenzy, and on this account was she sent for the despoiling of the Rulers who brought the World into being; and the Angels themselves went to war on her account; and while she experienced nothing, they set to work to mutually slaughter each other on account of the desire which she infused into them for herself.

Theodoret briefly follows Irenæus.

In these contradictory accounts we have a great confusion between the rôles played by Nous and Epinoia, the Father and Thought, the Spirit and Spiritual Soul. Then again how did the Lower Regions come into existence, for Epinoia to descend to them? This lacuna is filled by the fuller information of the *Philosophumena* which shows us the scheme of self-emanation out or down into matter by similitude, thus confining the problem of "evil" to space and time, and not raising it into an eternal principle. Naturally it is not to be supposed that the origin of "evil" is solvable for man in his present state, therefore whether it was according to the design or contrary to the design of the Father, will ever depend upon the point of view from which we severally regard the problem.

Law, Justice, and Compassion are not incompatible terms to one whose heart is set firm on spiritual things; and the view that evil is not a thing in itself, but exists only because of human ignorance, is one that must commend itself to the truly religious and philosophical mind. Thus evil is not a fixed quantity in itself, it depends on the internal attitude each man holds with regard to externals as to whether they are evil or no.

For instance, it is not evil for an animal or savage to kill, for the light of the higher law is not yet flaming brightly in their hearts. That only is evil if we do what is displeasing to the Self. This may perhaps throw some light on the Simonian dogma of action by accident (*ex accidenti*), or institution (θεσει), as opposed to action according to nature (*naturaliter* or φυσει)—evidently the same idea as the teaching of Heracleitus to act according to nature (κατα φυσιν) which he explains as according to the Unmanifested Harmony which we can hear by straining our ears to catch that still small voice within, the Voice of the Silence, the Logos or Self. Simon presumably refers to this in the phrase "the things which sound within" (τα ενηχα), an idea remarkably confirmed by Psellus,[129] who quotes the following Logion:

When thou seest a most holy, formless Fire shining and bounding throughout the depths of the whole Cosmos, give ear to the Voice of the Fire.

This brings us to a consideration of the teachings of Simon with regard to the Lesser World, the Microcosm, Man, and to the scheme of his soteriology. Evidently Simon taught the ancient, immemorial doctrine that the Microcosm Man was the Mirror and Potentiality of the Cosmos, the Macrocosm, as we have already seen above. Whatever was true of the emanation of the Universe, was also true of Man, whatever was true of the Macrocosmic Aeons was true of the Microcosmic Aeons in Man, which are potentially the same as those of the Cosmos, and will develop into the power and grandeur of the latter, if they can find suitable expression, or a fit vehicle. This view will explain the reason of the ancients for saying that we could only perceive that of which we have a germ already within us. Thus it is that Empedocles taught:

By earth earth we perceive; by water, water; by aether, aether; fire, by destructive fire; by friendship, friendship; and strife by bitter strife.

And if the potentiality of all resided in every man, the teaching on this point most forcibly has been, *Qui se cognoscit, in se omnia cognoscit*—He who knows himself, knows all in himself—as Q. Fabius Pictor tells us. And, therefore, the essential of moral and spiritual training in ancient times was the attainment of Self-Knowledge—that is to say, the attainment of the certitude that there is a divine nature within every man, which is of infinite capacity to absorb universal Wisdom; that, in brief, Man was *essentially* one with Deity.

With Simon, as with the Hermetic philosophers of ancient Egypt, all things were interrelated by correspondence, analogy, and similitude. "As above, so below," is the teaching on the Smaragdine Table of Hermes. Therefore, whatever happened to the divine Epinoia, the Supreme Mother, among the Aeons, happened also to the human Spiritual Soul or Monadic Essence, in its evolution through all stages of manifestation. This Soul is shut into all forms and bodies, successively up to the stage of man.

From one point of view this teaching has been conclusively proved by Modern Science. The evolution of the external form has been traced throughout all the kingdoms and is no longer in question. The ancient teachers of evolution, though less exact in detail, were more accurate in fact, in postulating a "something within" which alone could make the external evolution of form of any intelligible purpose. The Spiritual Soul—the Life, Consciousness, Spirit, Intelligence, whatever we may choose to call it—was formless in itself, but ever assuming new forms by a process called metempsychosis, metasomatosis, metangismos, etc., which in the human stage becomes reïncarnation, the rebirth or Punarjanman of the Hindûs.

So much has been written on metempsychosis and reïncarnation of late that it is hardly necessary to dwell on a now so familiar idea. In its widest sense the whole process of nature is subject to this mode of existence, and in its more restricted sense it is the path of pilgrimage of the Soul in the desert of Matter. In treating of a philosophical conception, which has already been completely established as far as its "visible side" is concerned by the researches of Modern Science in the field of evolution, it is a waste of time to obscure the main issue by a rehashing of the superstitious belief that the human Soul might pass back to the brute. It may be that this superstition arose from the consideration that the body and lower vestures of the Soul were shed off and gradually absorbed by the lower creation in the alchemical processes of nature. This was the fate of the "Purgations" of the Soul, but the Soul itself when once it had passed from bodies of the lower kingdoms, to bodies in the man-stage, could not retrogress beyond the limits of that human kingdom.

By a glance at the Diagram, and regarding it from the microcosmic point of view, it is easy to see that the inner nature of man is more complex than the elementary trichotomy of Body, Soul, and Spirit, might lead us to suppose. Each plane of Being, for which the Soul has its own appropriate Vesture, is generated from an "indivisible point," as Simon called it, a zero-point, to use a term of modern Chemistry; six of which are shown in the Diagram, and each plane of Being is bounded by such zero-points, for they are points like that of the Circle whose centre is everywhere and circumference nowhere.

To pass on to the soteriology of Simon. The general concept of this presents no difficulty to the student of Eastern Religions. The idea that the great teachers are Avatâras, incarnations, or descents, of the Supreme Being, appearing on earth to aid mankind, is simple enough to comprehend in itself, and would be open to little objection, were it not for the theological dogmas and mythological legends that are wont to be so busily woven round the lives of such teachers. In the present age it is hardly necessary for us, with the experience of the past before our eyes, to raise dissension as to whether such a manifestation is entirely divine, or entirely human, or perfectly human and divine at one and the same time, or neither or all of these.

Eastern philosophy, regarding not only the external phenomenal world as ever-changing and impermanent, but also all appearance or manifestation—no matter how subjective it may be to us now—as not the one Truth in itself, which it claims alone to be without change, it is easy to see the reason why the Gnostic Philosophers for the most part held to Doceticism—that is to say that the body of a Saviour was not the Saviour himself, but an appearance. The heat of polemical controversy may have led to exaggerated views on both sides, but the philosophical mind will not be distressed at the thought that the body is an appearance or mask of the real man, and that it forms no part of his eternal possession. None the less the body is real to us here, for we all have bodies of a like nature, and appearances are real to appearances. Yet this does not invalidate the further consideration that there are other bodies, vestures, or vehicles of consciousness, besides the gross physical "coat of skin," for the use of the spiritual man, each being an "appearance" in comparison to the higher vehicle, which is in its turn an "appearance" to that which is more subtle and less material or substantial than itself.

Thus, in the descent from the Divine World, the Soul transforms itself, or clothes itself in forms, or bodies, or vestures, which it weaves out of its own substance, like to the Powers of the Worlds it passes through, for every Soul has a different vehicle of consciousness for every World or Plane.

But the doctrine of the Soter, or Saviour, does not apply until the Christ-stage or consummation is reached. Following the idea of rebirth, there is a spiritual life cycle, or life-thread, on which the various earth-lives are strung, as beads on a necklace, each successive life being purer and nobler, as the Soul gains control of matter, or the driver control of the chariot and steeds that speed him through the experiences of life. As the end of this great cycle approaches, an earthly vehicle is evolved that can show forth the divine spirit in all the fulness possible to this world or phase of evolution.

Now as the problem can be viewed from either the internal or external point of view, we have the mystery of the Soul depicted both from the side of the involution of spirit into matter and of the evolution of matter into spirit. If, on the one hand, we insist too strongly on one view, we shall only have a one-sided conception of the process; if, on the other, we neglect one factor, we shall never solve the at present unknown quantity of the equation. Thus the Soul is represented as the "lost sheep" struggling in the meshes of the net of matter, passing from body to body, and the Spirit is represented as descending, transforming itself through the spheres, in order to finally rescue its Syzygy from the bonds that are about her.

The Soul aspires to the Spirit and the Spirit takes thought for the Soul; as the Simonians expressed it:

The male (Heaven, i.e., the Nous or Christ, or Spiritual Soul) looks down from above and takes thought for its co-partner (or Syzygy); while the Earth (i.e., the Epinoia or Jesus, or Human Soul) from below receives from the Heaven the intellectual (in the spiritual and philosophical sense, of course) fruits that come down to it and are cognate with the Earth (i.e., of the same nature essentially as Epinoia, who is essentially one with Nous).

When this mystery is represented dramatically, so to say, and personified, these two aspects of the Soul are depicted as two persons. Thus we have Simon and Helen, his favourite disciple, Krishna and Arjuna, etc. In the Canonical Gospels the favourite disciple is said to be John, and the women-disciples are placed well in the background. In the Gnostic Gospels, however, the women-disciples are not so ostracized, and the view taken by these early communities of philosophical and mystical Christians throws much light on that wonderful history of the Magdalene that has so touched the heart of Christendom. For instance, in the *Pistis-Sophia*, the chief of all the disciples, the most spiritual and intuitive, is Mary Magdalene. This is not without significance when we remember the love of the Christ for Mary "out of whom he had cast *seven* devils."

The allegory is a striking one, and perfectly comprehensible to the student of comparative religion. As there are seven Aeons in the Spiritual World, seven principles or aspects of the Spiritual Soul, so here on Earth, by analogy, there are seven lower aspects, or impure reflections. As there are seven Cardinal Virtues, the Prajnâ-Pâramitâs, or Perfections of Wisdom, of the Buddhists, so there are seven Cardinal Vices, and these must be cast out by the spiritual will, before the repentant Mary, or Human Soul, can be purified.

This is the mystery of the Helen, the "lost sheep." Then follows the mystical marriage of the Lamb, the union of the Human and Spiritual Soul in man, referred to so often in the Gospels and other mystical scriptures.

Naturally the language used is symbolical, and has naught to do with sex, in any sense. Woe unto him or her who takes these allegories of the Soul as literal histories, for nothing but sorrow will follow such materialization of divine mysteries. If Simon or his followers fell into this error, they worked their own downfall, under the Great Law, as surely do all who forge such bonds of matter for their own enslavement.

But with condemnation we have nothing to do; they alone who are without sin have the *right* to cast stones at the Magdalenes of this world; and they who are truly without sin use their purity to cleanse their fellows, and do not sully it with the stains of self-righteous condemnation. We, ordinary men and women of the age, are all "lost sheep," human souls struggling in ignorance; shall we then stone our fellows because their theology has a different nomenclature to our own? For man was the same in the past as he is to-day. The Human Soul has ever the same hopes and fears, loves and hates, passions and aspirations, no matter how the mere form of their expression differs. That which is important is the attitude we hold to the forms with which we are surrounded. To-day the form of our belief is changed; the fashion of our dress is scientific and not allegorical, but are we any nearer the realization that it is a dress and no more, and not the real expression of the true man within?

Let us now take a brief glance at the Symbolical Tree of Life, which plays so important a part in the Simonian Gnôsis. Not, however, that it was peculiar to this system, for several of the schools use the same symbology. For instance, in the *Pistis-Sophia*[130] the idea is immensely expanded, and there is much said of an Aeonian Hierarchy called the Five Trees. As this, however, may have been a later development, let us turn to the ancient Hindû Shâstras, and select one out of the many passages that could be adduced, descriptive of the Ashvattha Tree, the Tree of Life, "the Ashvattha of golden wings," where the bird-souls get their wings and fly away happily, as the *Sanatsujátîya* tells us. The passage we choose is from the *Bhagavad Gîtâ*, that marvellous philosophical episode from the *Mahâbhârata*, which from internal evidence, and at the very lowest estimate, must be placed at a date anterior to Simon. At the beginning of the fifteenth Adyâya we read:

They say the imperishable Ashvattha is with root above and branches below, of which the sacred hymns are the leaves. Who knows this, he is a knower of knowledge. Upwards and downwards stretch its branches, expanded by the potencies (Gunas); the sense-objects are its sprouts. Downwards, too, its roots are stretched, constraining to action in the world of men. Here neither its form is comprehended, nor its end, nor beginning, nor its support. Having cut with the firm sword of detachment (*sc.* non-attachment to the fruit of action) this Ashvattha, with its overgrown roots, then should he (the disciple) search out that Supreme whither they who come never return again, (with the thought) that now he is come to that primal Being, whence the evolution of old was emanated.

For what is this "sword of detachment" but another aspect of the "fiery sword" of Simon, which is turned about to guard the way to the Tree of Life? This "sword" is our passions and desires, which now keep us from the golden-leaved Tree of Life, whence we may find wings to carry us to the "Father in Heaven." For once we have conquered Desire and turned it into spiritual Will, it then becomes the "Sword of Knowledge"; and the way to the Tree of Spiritual Life being gained, the purified Life becomes the "Wings of the Great

Bird" on which we mount, to be carried to its Nest, where peace at last is found.

The simile of the Tree is used in many senses, not the least important of which is that of the heavenly "vine" of the reïncarnating Soul, every "life" of which is a branch. This explains Simon's citation of the Logion so familiar to us in the *Gospel according to Luke*:

Every tree not bearing good fruit is cut down and cast into the fire.

This also explains one of the inner meanings of the wonderful passage in the *Gospel according to John*:

I am the true vine and my Father is the husbandman. Every branch in me that beareth not fruit he taketh away; and every branch that beareth fruit he purgeth it that it may bear more fruit.[131]

For only the spiritual fruit of every life is harvested in the "Storehouse" of the Divine Soul; the rest is shed off to be purified in the "Fire" of earthly existence.

Into the correspondence between the world-process of Nature, and that which takes place in the womb of mortal woman, it will not be necessary to enter at length. No doubt Simon taught many other correspondences between the processes of Cosmic Nature and Microcosmic Man, but what were the details of this teaching we can in no way be certain. Simon may have made mistakes in physiology, according to our present knowledge, but with the evidence before us all we can do is to suspend our judgment. For in the first place, we do not know that he has been correctly reported by his patristic antagonists, and, in the second, we are even yet too ignorant of the process of the nourishment of the foetus to pronounce any *ex cathedrâ* statement. In any case Simon's explanation is more in agreement with Modern Science than the generality of the phantasies on scientific subjects to which the uninstructed piety of the early Fathers so readily lent itself. As to whether the Initiated of the ancients did or did not know of the circulation of the blood and the functions of the arterial system, we must remain in doubt, for both their well known method of concealing their knowledge and also the absence of texts which may yet be discovered by the industry of modern exploration teach us to hold our judgment in suspense.

Again, seeing the importance which the symbolical Tree played in the Simonian System, it may be that there was an esoteric teaching in the school, which pointed out correspondences in the human body for mystical purposes, as has been the custom for long ages in India in the Science of Yoga. In the human body are *at least* two "Trees," the nervous, and vascular systems. The former has its "root" above in the cerebrum, the latter has its roots in the heart. Along the trunks and branches run currents of "nervous ether" and "life" respectively, and the Science of Yoga teaches its disciples to use both of these forces for mystical purposes. It is highly probable also that the Gnostics taught the same processes to their pupils, as we know for a fact that the Neo-Platonists inculcated like practices. From these considerations, then, it may be supposed that Simon was not so ignorant of the real laws of the circulation of the blood as might otherwise be imagined; and as to the nourishment of the embryo, modern authorities are at loggerheads, the majority, however, inclining to the opinion of Simon, that the foetus is nourished through the umbilical cord.[132]

The last point of importance to detain us, before passing on to a notice on the magical practices ascribed to Simon, is the allegorical use made by the Simonians of Scripture. Here again we have little to do with the details reported, but only with the idea. It was a common belief of the sages of antiquity that the mythological part of the sacred writings of the nations were to be understood in an allegorical fashion. Not to speak of India, we have the Neo-Platonic School with its analogetical methods of interpretation, and the mention of a work of Porphyry in which an allegorical interpretation of the *Iliad* was attempted. Allegorical shows of a similar nature also were enacted in the Lesser Mysteries and explained in the Greater, as Julian tells us in the *Mother of the Gods*,[133] and Plutarch on the *Cessation of Oracles*.[134]

Much evidence could be adduced that this was a widespread idea held by the learned of antiquity, but space does not here allow a full treatment of the subject. What is important to note is that Simon claimed this as a method of his School, and therefore, in dealing with his system, we cannot leave out so important a factor, and persist in taking allegorical and symbolical expressions as literal teachings. We may say that the method is misleading and has led to much superstition among the ignorant, but we have no right to criticize the literal and historical meaning of an allegory, and then fancy that we have criticized the doctrine it enshrines. This has been the error of all rationalistic critics of the world bibles. They have wilfully set on one side the whole method of ancient religious teaching, and taken as literal history and narrative what was essentially allegorical and symbolical. Perhaps the reason for this may be in the fact that wherever religion decays and ignorance spreads herself, there the symbolical and allegorical is materialized into the historical and literal. The spirit is forgotten, the letter is deified. Hence the reäction of the rationalistic critic against the materialism and literalism of sacred verities. Nevertheless, such criticism does not go deep enough to affect the real truths of religion and the convictions of the human soul, any more than an aesthetic criticism on the shape of the Roman letters and Arabic figures can affect the truth of an algebraical formula. Rationalistic criticism may stir people from literalism and dogmatic crystallization, in fact it has done much in this way, but it does not reach the hidden doctrines.

Now Simon contended that many of the narrations of Scripture were allegorical, and opposed those who held to the dead-letter interpretation. To the student of comparative religion, it is difficult to see what is so highly blameworthy in this. On the contrary, this view is so worthy of praise, that it deserves to be widely adopted today, at the latter end of the nineteenth century. To understand antiquity, we must follow the methods of the wise among the ancients, and the method of allegory and parable was the manner of teaching of the great Masters of the past.

But supposing we grant this, and admit that all Scriptures possess an inner meaning and lend themselves to interpretation on every plane of being and thought, who is to decide whether any particular interpretation is just or no? Already we have writers arising, giving diametrically opposite interpretations of the same mystical narrative, and though this may be an advance on bald physical literalism, it is by no means encouraging to the instructed and philosophical mind.

If the Deity is no respecter of persons, times, or nations, and if no age is left without witness of the Divine, it would seem to be in accordance with the fitness of things that all religions in their purity are one in essence, no matter how overgrown with error they may have become through the ignorance of man. If, again, the root of true Religion is one, and the nature of the Soul and of the inner constitution of things is identical in all climes and times, as far as its *main features* are concerned, no matter what terminology, allegory, and symbology may be employed to describe it; and not only this, but if it be true that such subjective things are as potent facts in human consciousness as any that exist, as indeed is evidenced by the unrivalled influence such things have had on human hearts and actions throughout the history of the world—then we must consider that an interpretation that fits only one system and is found entirely unsuitable to the rest, is no part of universal religion, and is due rather to the ingenuity of the interpreter than to a discovery of any law of subjective nature. The method of comparative religion alone can give us any certainty of correct interpretation, and a refusal to institute such a comparison should invalidate the reliability of all such enquiries.

Now Simon is reported to have endeavoured to find an inner meaning in scriptural narratives and mythologies, and against this method we can have nothing to say; it is only when a man twists the interpretation to suit his own prejudices that danger arises. Simon, however, is shown to have appealed to the various sacred literatures known in his time, an eclectic and theosophical method, and one that cannot very well be longer set on one side even in our own days.

The primitive church was not so forgetful of symbology as are the majority of the Christian faith to-day. One of the commonest representations of primitive Christian art was that of the "Four Rivers." As the Rev. Professor Cheetham tells us:

We find it repeated over and over again in the catacombs, either in frescoes or in the sculptured ornaments of sarcophagi, and sometimes on the bottoms of glass cups which have been discovered therein.[135]

The interpretations given by the early divines were many and various; in nearly every case, however, it was an interpretation which applied to the Christian system alone, and accentuated external differences. Little attempt was made to find an interpretation in nature, either objective or subjective, or in man. Simon, at any rate, made the attempt—an effort to broaden out into a universal system applying to all men at all times. This is also the real spirit of pure Christianity which is so often over-clouded by theological partisanship. A true interpretation must stand the test of not only religious aspiration, but also philosophical thought and scientific observation.

Nor again should we find cause to grieve at an attempted interpretation of the Trojan Horse, that was fabricated by the advice of Athena (Minerva-Epinoia), for did not George Stanley Faber, in the early years of this century, labour with much learning to prove its identity with the Ark. True he only turned similar myths into the terms of one myth and got no further, but that was an advance on his immediate predecessors. Simon, however, had centuries before gone further than Faber, as far as theory is concerned, by seeking an interpretation in nature. But, in his turn, as far as our records go, he only attempted the interpretation of one aspect of this graphic symbol, saying that it typified "ignorance." An interpretation, however, to be complete should cover all planes of consciousness and being from the physical human plane to the divine cosmic. The Ark floating on the Waters of the Deluge and containing the Germs of Life, the Mundane Egg in the Waters of Space, and the Mare with her freight of armed warriors, all typify a great fact in nature, which may be studied scientifically in the development of the germ-cell, and ethically by analogy, as the egg of ignorance, the germs in which are, from the lower aspect, our own evil passions.

In speaking of such allegories and tracing the correspondences between certain symbologies and the natural facts of embryology, Simon speaks of the "cave" which plays so important a part in so many religious allegories. As the child is born in a "cave," so the "new man" is also born in a "cave," and all the Saviours are so recorded to have been born in their birth legends. The Mysteries of antiquity were for the most part solemnized in caves, or rock-cut temples. The Epoptæ deemed such caverns as symbols both of the physical world and Hades or the Unseen World, which surrounds every child of man. Into such a cave, in the middle of the Ocean, Cronus shut his children, as Porphyry[136] tells us. It was called by the name Petra, or Rock, and from such a Rock Mithras is said to have been born.[137]

Faber endeavours to identify this symbolical cave with the Ark,[138] which may be permissible from one aspect, as the womb of mother nature and of the human mother correspond analogically.

In the "new birth" of the mysteries, the Souls were typified as bees born from the body of an ox, for they were to gather the honey of wisdom, and were born from the now dead body of their lower natures. In the cave were two doors, one for immortals, the other for mortals. In this connection the cave is the psychic womb that surrounds every man, of which Nicodemus displays such ignorance in the Gospels. It is the microcosmic Middle Distance; by one door the Lower Soul enters, and uniting with its immortal consort, who descends through the door of the immortals, becomes immortal.

The cavern is overshadowed by an olive tree—again the Tree of Life to which we have referred above—on the branches of which the doves rest, and bring back the leaves to the ark of the body and the prisoner within it.

But space does not permit us to pursue further this interesting subject, which requires an entire treatise by itself, or even a series of volumes. Enough, however, has been said to show that the method of interpretation employed by Simon is not without interest and profit, and that the tolerant spirit of to-day which animates the best minds and hearts in Christendom will find no reason to mete out to Simon wholesale condemnation on this score.

There are also many other points of interest that could be elaborated upon, in the fragments of the system we are reviewing, but as my task is in the form of an essay, and not an exhaustive work, I must be content to pass them by for the present, and to hurry on to a few words on that strange and misunderstood subject, commonly known as Magic.

What Magic, the "Great Art" of the ancients, was in reality is now as difficult to discover as is the true Religion that underlies all the great religions of the world. It was an art, a practice, the Great and Supreme Art of the most Sacred Science of God, the Universe and Man. It was and it is all this in its highest sense, and its method was what is now called "creation." As the Aeons imitated the Boundless Power and emanated or created in their turn, so could man imitate the Aeons and emanate or create in his turn. But "creation" is not generation, it is a work of the "mind," in the highest sense of the word. By purification and aspiration, by prayer and fasting, man had to make his mind harmonious with the Great Mind of the Universe, and so by imitation create pure vehicles whereby his consciousness could be carried in every direction of the Universe. Such spiritual operations required the greatest purity and piety, real purity and true piety, without disguise or subterfuge, for man had to face himself and his God, before whom no disguise was possible. The most secret motives, the most hidden desires, were revealed by the stern self-discipline to which the Adepts of the Science subjected themselves.

But as in all things here below, so with the Art of Magic, it was two-fold. Above I have only spoken of the bright side of it, the path along which the World-Saviours have trodden, for no one can gain entrance to the path of self-sacrifice and compassion unless his heart burns with love for all that lives, and unless he treads the way of wisdom only in order that he may become that Path itself for the salvation of the race. But there is the other side; knowledge is knowledge irrespective of the use to which it may be put. The sword of knowledge is two-edged, as remarked above, and may be put to good or evil use, according to the selfishness or unselfishness of the possessor.

But *corruptio optimi pessima,* and as the employment of wisdom for the benefit of mankind—as, for instance, curing the sick, physically and morally—is the highest, so the use of any abnormal power for the advantage of self is the vilest sin that man can commit.

There are strange analogies in Nature, and the higher the spiritual, the lower the corresponding material process; so that we find in the history of magic—perhaps the longest history in the world—extremes ever meeting. Abuse of spiritual powers, and the vilest physical processes, noxious, fantastic, and pestilential, are recorded in the pages of so-called magical literature, but such foul deeds are no more real Magic than are the horrors of religious fanaticism the outcome of true Mohammedanism or Christianity. This is the abuse, the superstition, the degeneration of all that is good and true, rendered all the more vile because it pertains to denser planes of matter than even the physical. It is a strange thing that the highest should pair with the lowest where man is concerned, but it ever remains true that the higher we climb the lower we may fall.

Man is much the same in nature at all times, and though the Art was practised in its purity by the great World-Teachers and their immediate followers, whether we call it by the name Magic or no, it ever fell into abuse and degeneracy owing to the ingrained ignorance and selfishness of man. Thus the Deity and Gods or Daemons of one nation became the Devil and Demons of another; the names were changed, the facts remained the same. For if we are to reject all such things as superstition, hallucination, and what not, the good must go with the bad. But facts, whether good or bad, are still facts, and man is still man, no matter how he changes the fashion of his belief. The followers of the World-Teachers cannot hold to the so-called "miracles" of their respective Masters and reject all others as false in fact, no matter from what source they may believe they emanate. In nature there can be nothing supernatural, and as man stands mid-way between the divine and infernal, if we accept the energizing of the one side of his nature, we must also accept that of the other. Both are founded on nature and science, both are under law and order.

The great Master of Christendom is reported to have told his disciples that if they had but faith they should do greater works than even he had done. Either this was false or else the followers have been false to their Teacher. There is no escape from the dilemma. And such "works" are to be wrought by divine Magic alone, or if the term be disliked, by whatever name the great Science of the Soul and Divine things may be called.

For the last two hundred years or so it has been the fashion to deride all such matters, perhaps owing to a reäction against over-credulity on the part of those who held to the letter of the law and forgot its spirit; but to-day it is no longer possible to entirely set aside this all-important part of man's nature, and it now calls for as strict a scientific treatment as the facts of the physical universe have been subjected to.

Hypnotism, Mesmerism, Spiritualism and Psychical Research, are the cloud no bigger than a man's hand that is forcing the facts of Magic again on the attention of both the theological and scientific world. Hypnotism and Psychical Research are already becoming respectable and attracting the attention of the generality of men of science and of our clergy. Spiritualism and Mesmerism are still tabooed, but wait their turn for popular recognition, having already been recognized by pioneers distinguished in science and other professions.

Of course I speak only of the facts of these arts, I do not speak of the theories put forward.

All these processes are in the very outermost court of the Temple of True Magic, even if they are not outside the precinct. But they are sufficient for our purpose, and should make the serious thinker and unprejudiced enquirer pause before pronouncing the words, superstition and hallucination, in too confident a tone, for he now must see the necessity of having a clear idea of what he means by the terms.

It is not uncommon of late to hear the superficially instructed setting down everything to "suggestion," a word they have picked up from modern hypnotic research, or "telepathy," a name invented by psychical research—the ideas being as old as the world—forgetting that their mind remains in precisely the same attitude with regard to such matters as it was in previously when they utterly denied the possibility of suggestion and telepathy. But to the earnest and patient student hypnotism and the rest are but the public reäppearance of what has always existed in spite of the denial of two hundred years or so, and instead of covering the whole ground is but the forward spray from the returning wave of psychism which will sweep the nations off their feet and moral balance, if they will not turn to the experience of the past and gain strength to withstand the inrush.

The higher forms of all these things, in the Western World, should have now been in the hands of the ministers of the Church, in which case we should not have had the reäppearance of such powers in the hands of vulgar stage exhibitions and mercenary public mediumship.

But so it is; and in vain is it any longer to raise the cry of fraud and hallucination on the one hand and of the devil on the other. This is a mere shirking of responsibility, and nothing but a reasonable investigation and an insistence on the highest ideals of life will help humanity.

I do not intend to enter into any review of the "wonders" attributed to Simon, neither to deny them as hallucinations, nor attribute them to the devil, nor explain them away by "suggestion." As a matter of fact we do not even know whether Simon did or pretended to do any of the precise things mentioned. All we are competent to decide is the general question, viz., that any use of abnormal power is pernicious if done for a personal motive, and will assuredly, sooner or later, react on the doer.

Here and there in the patristic accounts we light on a fact worthy of consideration, as, for example, when Simon is reported to have denied that the real soul of a boy could be exorcised, and said that it was only a daemon, in this case a sub-human intelligence or elemental, as the Mediæval Kabalists called them. Again the Simonians are said to have expelled any from their Mysteries who worshipped the statues of Zeus or Athena as being representatives of Simon and Helen; thus showing that they were symbolical figures for some purpose other than ordinary worship; and probably the sect in its purity possessed a body of teaching which threw light on many of the religious practices of the times, and gave them a rational interpretation, quite at variance with the fantastic diabolism which the Fathers have so loudly charged against them.

The legends of magic are the same in all countries, fantastic enough to us in the nineteenth century, in all conscience, and most probably exaggerated out of all correct resemblance to facts by the excited imagination of the legend-tellers, but still it is not all imagination, and after sifting out even ninety-nine per cent of rubbish, the residue that remains is such vast evidence to the main facts that it is fairly overwhelming, and deserves the investigation of every honest student.

But the study is beset with great difficulty, and if left in the hands of untrained thinkers, as are the majority of those who are interested in such matters in the present day, will only result in a new phase of credulity and superstition. And such a disastrous state of affairs will be the distinct fault of the leaders of thought in the religious, philosophical, and scientific world, if they refuse the task which is naturally theirs, and if they are untrue to the responsibility of their position as the directors, guardians, and adjusters of the popular mind. Denial is useless, mere condemnation is of small value, explanation alone will meet the difficulty.

Thus when we are brought face to face with the recital of magical wonders as attributed to Simon in the patristic legends, it is not sufficient to sweep them on one side and ticket them with the contemptuous label of "superstition." We must recognize that whether or not these things were actually done by Simon, the ancient world both Pagan and Christian firmly believed in their reality, and that if our only attitude towards them is one of blank denial, we include in that denial the possibility of the so-called "miracles" of Christianity and other great religions, and therewith invalidate one of the most important factors of religious thought and history. That the present attitude of denial is owing to the absurd explanation of the phenomena given by the majority of the ancient worthies, is easily admissible, but this is no reason why the denial of the possibilities of the existence of such things should be logical or scientific.

As to the wonders ascribed to Simon, though extraordinary, they are puerile compared to the ideals of the truly religious mind, and if Simon used such marvels as proofs of the truth of his doctrine, he unduly took advantage of the ignorance of the populace and was untrue to his better nature.

Again, setting aside all historical criticism, if Simon, as the *Acts* report, thought to purchase spiritual powers with money, or that those who were really in possession of such powers would ever sell them, we can understand the righteous indignation of the apostles, though we cannot understand their cursing a brother-man. The view of the Christian writer on this point is a true one, but the dogma that every operation which is not done in the name of the particular Master of Christendom is of the Devil—or, to avoid personifications, is evil—can hardly find favour with those who believe in the brotherhood of the whole race and that Deity is one, no matter under what form worshipped.

Finally, to sum up the matter, we have cited our authorities, and reviewed them, and then endeavoured to sift out what is good from the heap, leaving the rubbish to its fate. Removed as we are by so many centuries from the fierce strife of religious controversy which so deeply marked the rise of Christianity, we can view the matter with impartiality and seek to redress the errors that are patent both on the side of orthodoxy and of heterodoxy. It is true we cannot be free of the past, but it is also true that to identify ourselves with the hates and strifes of the ancients, is merely to retrogress from the path of progress. On the contrary, our duty should be to identify ourselves with all that is good and beautiful and true in the past, and so gleaning it together, bind it into a sheaf of corn that, when ground in the mills of common-sense and practical experience, may feed the millions of every denomination who for the most part are starving on the unsatisfying husks of crude dogmatism. There is no need for a new revelation, in whatever sense the word is understood, but there is every need for an explanation of the old revelations and the undeniable facts of human experience. If the Augean stables of the materialism that is so prevalent in the religion, philosophy and science of to-day, are to be cleansed, the spiritual sources of the world-religions can alone be effectual for their cleansing, but these are at present hidden by the rocks and overgrowth of dogma and ignorance. And this overgrowth can only be removed by explanation and investigation, and each who works at the task is, consciously or unconsciously, in the train of the Hercules who is pioneering the future of humanity.

NOTES:

[96]

Julius Caesar, III. ii. 106-8.

[97]

Op. cit. i. 4. Compare the Diagram and explanation of the Middle Distance *infra.* The Moon is the "Lord" of the lower plane of the

Middle Distance, the Astral Light of the medieval Kabalists. This is a doctrine common to the Hermetic, Vedântic, and many other schools of Antiquity.

[98]

xi. 37.

[99]

Philos., ix. 10.

[100]

Zohar, i. 50*b*, Amsterdam and Brody Editions: quoted in Isaac Myer's *Qabbalah*, pp. 376, 377.

[101]

See Cory's *Ancient Fragments*, 2nd ed.; not the reëdited third edition, which is no longer Cory's work.

[102]

εισι παντα πυρος ενος εκγεγαωτα—*Psell. 24—Plet. 30.*

[103]

Proc. in Theol. 333—*in Tim.* 157.

[104]

πηγαιους κρατηρας—I have ventured the above translation for this difficult combination from the meaning of the term πηγη, found elsewhere in the Oracles, in the metaphorical sense of "source" (compare also Plato, *Phæd.* 245 C., 856 D., πηγη και αρχη χινησεως—"the source and beginning of motion"), and also from the meaning of κρατηρ (*cratêr*), as "a cup-shaped hollow."

The idea of this Crater is interestingly exemplified in the Twelfth Book of Hermes Trismegistus, called "His Crater, or Monas," as follows:

"10. *Tat.* But wherefore, Father, did not God distribute the Mind to all men?

"11. *Herm.* Because it pleased him, O Son, to set that in the middle among all souls, as a reward to strive for.

"12. *Tat.* And where hath he set it?

"13. *Herm.* Filling a large Cup or Bowl (Crater) therewith, he sent it down, giving also a Cryer or Proclaimer.

"14. And he commanded him to proclaim these things to the souls of men.

"15. Dip and wash thyself, thou that art able, in this Cup or Bowl: Thou that believeth that thou shalt return to him that sent this cup; thou that acknowledgest whereunto thou wert made.

"16. As many, therefore, as understood the Proclamation, and were *baptized*, or dowsed into the *Mind*, these were made partakers of knowledge, and became perfect men, receiving the Mind."

This striking passage explains the mystic "Baptism of Fire," or Mind, whereby man became one with his Divine Monas, which is indeed his "Mother Vortex" or Source.

[105]

Proc. in Parm.

[106]

Proc. in Theol. Plat., 171, 172.

[107]

Proc. in Tim., 167.

[108]

Proc. in Theol., 321.

[109]

Proc. in Crat.

[110]

Dionys., xiv.

[111]

Præp. Evan., i. 10.

[112]

The names of these seven flames of the Fire, with their surface translations, are as follows: Kâlî, Dark-blue; Karâlî, Terrible; Mano-javâ, Swift as Thought; Su-lohitâ, Deep-red colour; Su-dhûmra-varnâ, Deep-purple colour; Ugrâ or Sphulinginî, Hot, Passionate, or

Sparkling; Pradîptâ, Shining, Clear. These are the literal meanings; the mystic meanings are very different, and among other things denote the septenary prismatic colours and other septenaries in nature.

[113]

Hibbert lectures, 1887: "Lecture on the Origin and Growth of Religion as illustrated by the Religion of the Ancient Babylonians," pp. 179, 180.

[114]

See Schwartze's *Pistis-Sophia* and Amélineau's *Notice sur le Papyrus Gnostique Bruce.*

[115]

De Mysteriis Liber, vii. 4.

[116]

Compare also *Herodot.* ii, 54—φονη ανθρωπηιη.

[117]

Lib. v.

[118]

Psel. 7.

[119]

Psel. Schol. in Orac. Magic, p. 70.

[120]

Theodoret gives εννοια.

[121]

A. Aphthartos Morphê. B. Nous tôn Holôn. c. Epinoia Megalê. D. Eikôn. a. Nous. b. Phônê. c. Logismos. d. Enthumêsis. e. Onoma. f. Epinoia.

[122]

xi. 47.

[123]

Ibid., xi. 18, 38.

[124]

Wilson's Trans. i. pp. 55 *et seqq.*

[125]

Prabhavâpyaya: Pra-bhava=the forth-being or origin, and Apy-aya=the return or reabsorption. It is the same idea as the Simonian Treasure-house.

[126]

Ayana simply means "moving."

[127]

Mânava-Dharma Shâstra, i. 10.

[128]

Op. cit., iv. 251.

[129]

14.

[130]

This Gnostic gospel, together with the treatises entitled, *The Book of the Gnoses of the Invisible* and *The Book of the Great Logos in each Mystery* (the Bruce MSS.), is especially referred to, as, with the exception of the *Codex Nazaræus,* being the only Gnostic works remaining to us. All else comes from the writings of the Fathers.

[131]

xv, 1, 2

[132]

The most advanced theory, however, is that the foetus derives nourishment from the amniotic fluid, and Dr. Jerome A. Anderson sums up his highly interesting paper on the "Nutrition of the Foetus" in the *American Journal of Obstetrics,* Vol. XXI, July, 1888, as follows:

"To briefly sum up the facts supporting amniotic nutrition:

"1st. The constant presence of nutritive substances in the amniotic fluid during the whole period of gestation.

"2nd. The certainty of the absorption by a growing, almost skinless, foetus of any nutritive material in which it is constantly bathed.

"3rd. The permeability of the digestive tract at an early period, and the necessary entrance therein, according to the laws of hydrostatics, of the albuminous amniotic fluid.

"4th. The presence of, as it seems to me, *bonâ fide* débris of digestion, or meconium, in the lower intestine.

"5th. The presence of urine in the bladder, and bile in the upper intestine; their normal locations.

"6th. The mechanical difficulties opposing direct nutrition through the placenta, and the impossibility of nourishment by this method during the early stages of embryonic life previous to the formation of the placenta or umbilical vesicle.

"7th. The evident material source of the fluid, as shown by the hydrorrheas of pregnancy, as well as in the exhaustion the mother experiences, in some cases, at least, under its loss and rapid reproduction.

"8th. The entire absence during gestation of any trace of the placenta in certain animals, notably the salamander."

[133]

Oratio V, *In Matrem Deorum.*

[134]

De Defectu Oraculorum, xxi.

[135]

Dictionary of Christian Antiquities, art. "Four Rivers, The."

[136]

The Homeric Cave of Nymphs, περι του εν Οδυσσεια των Νυμφων αντρου.

[137]

λεγουσιν εκ πετρας γεγεννησθαι αυτον—Just. Mart. *Dial. cum. Tryph.*

[138]

Cabiri, ii, 363.